IGRAINE
THE
BRAVE

IGRAINE
THE
BRAVE

by

Cornelia Funke
With illustrations by the author

Translated from the
German by Anthea Bell

Chicken House

First published in Germany as Igraine Ohnefurcht
Original text copyright © 1998 by Cecilie Dressler Verlag, Hamburg,
Germany
English translation by Anthea Bell copyright © 2007 by Cornelia Funke
Inside illustrations © 1998 Cornelia Funke

First published in Great Britain in 2007 by
The Chicken House
2 Palmer Street
Frome, Somerset BA11 1DS
United Kingdom
www.doublecluck.com

Cover design by Ian Butterworth
Cover illustration by Nick Price © 2007
Inside design and typesetting by Ian Butterworth
Printed and bound in Great Britain

1 3 5 7 9 10 8 6 4 2

British Library Cataloguing in Publication data available.

ISBN 978 1 905294 45 9

IGRAINE

I love Igraine because she is so feisty. Whether it's
spells going wrong, annoying big brothers, finding
your castle is under siege, or having to dash off on
a quest at a moment's notice – she's up for it. But
Igraine's not pig-headed, she learns about true bravery,
and that it's not just about swords and fighting.
Cornelia Funke makes us laugh and learn a bit about
that too. In fact I might become more chivalrous!

Barry Cunningham
Publisher and Would-be Knight

Who's Who in Igraine the Brave

 **The Fair Melisande and Sir Lamorak the Wily** (sometimes known as Sir Lamorak the Witty) – the greatest magicians between the Whispering  Woods and the Giant's Hills. They live at Pimpernel Castle and have two children, Albert and Igraine.

Albert – oldest son of the house. He is training to be a magician like his parents.

 **Igraine** – younger sister to Albert. She longs to be a knight and is not interested in magic at all.

Sisyphus – Igraine's talking cat.

 Singing Books of Magic –
the most precious and sought-after
possession of Sir Lamorak and
the Fair Melisande.

 **Baroness of Darkrock** –
nearest neighbour to
the folk in Pimpernel Castle.

Bertram – Master of Horse to the Baroness.

 **Osmund the Greedy or Osmund the
Magnificent** (depends on who is talking!)
– nephew of the Baroness of Darkrock.

Rowan Heartless, who also goes by the names of **Spiky Knight** or **Iron Hedgehog** – a knight who is the castellan and ally of Osmund.

Lancelot – the Baroness's very fast and special horse.

Garleff – a red-headed giant.

The Sorrowful Knight of the Mount of Tears or **Sir Urban of Wintergreen** – a knight Igraine befriends. He teaches Igraine the rules of chivalry by which a knight lives (or let's say: by which he ought to live).

THE SORROWFUL KNIGHT'S RULES OF CHIVALRY

Help damsels in distress.

Never turn your fighting skills against weaker opponents.

Protect the weak.

Use your sword only in self-defence or defence of others — never to enrich yourself.

And most important: always remember that your opponent may not be keeping to the rules himself.

P.S. A knight can never lose his honour in a fair fight.

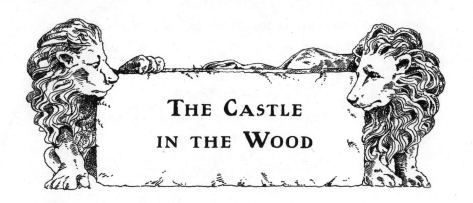

THE CASTLE
IN THE WOOD

Igraine woke up because something was crawling over
her face. Something with a lot of legs. She opened
her eyes and there it was, sitting right on the end
of her nose, a fat black spider. Igraine was scared stiff of
spiders.

'Sisyphus!' she whispered in a trembling voice. 'Wake
up, Sisyphus. Shoo that spider away!'

The cat raised his furry grey face from Igraine's
stomach, blinked, stretched – and snapped up the spider
from the end of her nose. One gulp, and it was gone.

'Did I say anything about eating it?' Igraine wiped
cat-spit off her cheek and pushed Sisyphus off her bed.
'A spider on my nose,' she muttered, throwing back the
covers. 'The day before my birthday too. That's not a
good omen.'

Barefoot, she went over to the window and looked out.
The sun was already high in the sky above Pimpernel
Castle. The tower cast its shadow over the courtyard,

doves were preening on the battlements, and a horse snorted down in the stables.

Pimpernel Castle had belonged to Igraine's family for more than three hundred years. Her mother's great-great-great-great-great-grandfather had built it. (There may have been a few more 'greats' in that; Igraine wasn't sure.) The castle was not large; it had only a single tower, which leaned over sideways, and the walls weren't much more than a metre thick, but Igraine thought it was the most beautiful castle in the world.

Wild flowers grew between the paving stones in the courtyard. Swallows nested under the roof of the tower in spring, and water snakes lived under the blue water lilies in the great castle moat. Two stone lions, high on a ledge above the gateway, guarded the castle. When Igraine scraped the moss off their manes they purred like cats, but if a stranger came near they bared their stony teeth and roared. They sounded so terrifying that even the wolves in the nearby forest hid.

The lions, though, were not the only guardians of Pimpernel. Stone gargoyles looked down from the walls and made terrible faces at any stranger. If you tickled their noses with a dove's feather they laughed so loud that the bird droppings crumbled off the castle battlements, but their wide mouths could swallow cannonballs, and they crunched up burning arrows as if there were nothing tastier in the world.

Luckily, however, the gargoyles hadn't had any arrows or cannonballs to eat for a long time. It was many years since Pimpernel Castle had been attacked. Once upon a time life hadn't been so peaceful. For Igraine's family owned the famous Singing Books of Magic, and many powerful men had wished to own them. Robber knights, dukes, barons, even two kings had attacked Pimpernel to steal the books. But they had all gone away empty-handed, and since Igraine's birth, life had been quiet at Pimpernel.

'Mmm, just smell that!' Igraine put Sisyphus down on the window sill beside her and took a deep breath of the

13

cool morning air. A delicious smell of wood ash, honey and vervain met her nostrils, and a shimmering pink glow rose into the sky from the top window of the tower. The magic workshop where Igraine's parents cast their spells lay behind that window, for noble Sir Lamorak and the Fair Melisande were the greatest magicians between the Whispering Woods and the Giant's Hills.

'Why are they working magic so early in the morning?' Igraine whispered anxiously into Sisyphus's pointy ear. 'I don't suppose they've even had breakfast yet. Do you think they're worried my present won't be ready in time?'

She quickly brushed a few moths off her woolly trousers, climbed into them, and put her great-grandfather's chain-mail shirt over her head. Igraine had worn it ever since she found it in the armoury, although it came down to her knees and she had to admit that it wasn't very comfortable. Her big brother Albert wanted to be a magician like their parents, but Igraine thought magic was dreadfully boring. Incantations, spells, lists of ingredients for magical powders and potions – learning all that by heart gave her a headache. No, she'd rather be like her great-grandfather Pelleas of Pimpernel. He was a knight who fought in tournaments and had adventures from morning till night – if the family stories were to be believed. Albert laughed at her ambition, but that's big brothers for you. Now and then Igraine took her revenge by putting woodlice in his magic coat.

'Laugh all you like!' she said when Albert teased her. 'You wait and see. I bet you ten of your tame mice I'll win one of the king's tournaments some day.'

Albert loved his mice, but he accepted Igraine's bet all the same. As for Sir Lamorak and the Fair Melisande, they always exchanged worried glances when their daughter came down to breakfast in her mail-shirt. Her family definitely didn't think much of her plans for the future.

'Come on, Sisyphus.' Igraine buckled up her belt and put the yawning tomcat under her arm. 'Let's go and do a bit of spying.' She ran downstairs to the Great Hall, passing the portraits of her ancestors (who all looked very glum), and pushed open the big gate leading into the courtyard. It was a lovely warm day. The scent of flowers filled the air within the high castle walls, mingling with the smell of mouse droppings.

'Oh, Sisyphus, Sisyphus!' said Igraine reproachfully as she carried the cat downstairs with her. 'If you lay off Albert's mice for much longer, we'll be treading on them when we cross the courtyard! Couldn't you at least scare them away now and then?'

'Too dangerous,' growled the cat, sleepily closing his eyes. Ever since Igraine had sprinkled him with Albert's red magic powder he'd been able to talk, though he didn't often feel like it.

'You're just a scaredy-cat,' said Igraine. 'Albert may keep threatening to turn you into a dog, but he'd never really do it. He doesn't know how. And even if he did – well, my parents would never let him.'

Sisyphus yawned in answer, and pretended to be asleep as she carried him over to the Enchanted Tower. The single tower of Pimpernel stood right in the middle of the castle courtyard, surrounded by a moat of its own, not as wide as the outer moat, but very deep. Igraine's ancestors had survived many a siege in this tower, because you could barricade yourself inside, even if the rest of the castle had been captured. The only way across the moat was over a very narrow bridge which could be raised in times of war. A dragon had once lived underneath (he hadn't been very big, but in the family chronicles he was known as the Knight-Eater). Igraine often wished he were still there, because now the underside of the bridge was infested with spiders. They made her knees shake when she went to visit her parents in their workshop. And as Albert knew that, he sometimes drew the bridge up just a bit so that she had to jump the gap. He'd done that today. Igraine cursed him, but she jumped, with Sisyphus under her arm.

'Quiet now!' she whispered as she crept over the bridge, her knees still all spidery-weak. 'No mewing, no hissing, no purring, nothing. You know Albert has ears like a bat.'

The cat just gave her a scornful look as she put him down outside the tower door. Of course. He could prowl about much more quietly than she could, but Igraine did her best. A few startled bats fluttered to meet them

when she climbed the endless staircase on tiptoe
– there were hundreds up in the rafters – and
Albert's tame mice sat on almost every step, but
Sisyphus acted as if he didn't even see them.

The heavy oak door of the workshop was
painted with magical signs, and the door handle
was a small brass serpent that liked to bite
strangers' hands.

Igraine cautiously put her ear to the door and
listened. She could hear the Books of Magic
singing very indistinctly in their high voices.
Sisyphus rubbed against her legs and purred. He
wanted his breakfast.

'What did I tell you?' whispered Igraine crossly,
pushing him away. 'Be quiet!'

But at that moment the door opened. Just a
crack, just wide enough for Albert to put his head
out.

'I might have known!' he said, smiling his what-
a-silly-little-sister smile. His nose was smudged
with wood ash, and there were two mice in his
hair.

'I was passing here entirely by chance,'
Igraine snapped at him. 'I just wanted to ask
when we're finally going to have breakfast.'

Albert's smile widened. 'You
won't find out what you really

want to know!' he said. 'Your birthday present has always been a surprise, and it's going to be a surprise this time too. Go and feed the snakes.'

Igraine stood on tiptoe so that she could at least steal a glance into the room over his shoulder, but Albert pushed her back.

'Go away and play knights in armour, little sister!' he said. 'I'll ring the bell for breakfast when we're ready.'

'Good morning, honey!' Igraine heard her mother call inside the magic workshop.

'Good morning!' called her father Sir Lamorak.

Igraine didn't answer. She stuck her tongue out at Albert and climbed down all those stairs again with her head held high.

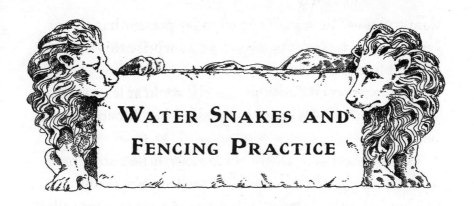

WATER SNAKES AND FENCING PRACTICE

Threw water snakes' food was in the kitchen, and half a dozen of Albert's mice scurried off the table as Igraine came in. They'd been at the cheese again, and when Sisyphus pushed his way past Igraine's legs they trotted past him as calmly as if he were stuffed. One of these days I'll catch them, thought Igraine, even if Albert does turn me into a spider for it. Albert! What use are brothers? Especially big brothers . . .

'The same old whispering every year, the same old hush-hush stuff,' she said crossly, putting a saucepan over the nibbled cheese to cover it. 'But they're really going too far this time! They've been up there working magic for five days now. Are they giving me an elephant or what?'

She poured some milk and water into Sisyphus's bowl, took the bucket of magic leftovers out of the oven, where her mother always left it to hide it from the mice, and carried it into the castle courtyard. Sisyphus followed her, with milk on his whiskers.

The great drawbridge squealed horribly when Igraine let it down. Of course. All this magic, but it never even occurred to anyone to oil the chain. Sisyphus brushed past her legs and put his head over the side of the bridge, looking for his breakfast. The fish in the large outer moat weren't under Albert's protection, and the cat was very fond of fish. It was little short of a miracle that there were still shoals of them left. Igraine took a couple of blue-shelled eggs out of the bucket of magic leftovers and threw them in among the water lilies.

The water around the flowers began moving at once, as five snakes reached their shimmering heads up to Igraine, tongues darting in and out.

'I'm terribly sorry,' she said, leaning down to them, 'but it's Albert's dry biscuits and blue eggs again today.'

The entire bucket was full of them. Even Igraine had to admit that Albert was quite a talented magician for someone of his age, but as soon as he tried to conjure up something edible, he produced only blue eggs and dry biscuits. However, water snakes aren't choosy, and as usual they devoured Albert's magical failures with the utmost relish. Meanwhile Igraine wandered to the far end of the bridge and looked across the marshy meadows beyond the castle. Apart from a few rabbits hopping through the grass, nothing stirred in the morning sunlight. Igraine sighed.

'Feeding the snakes every morning,' she muttered,

'dusting the Books of Magic on Wednesdays and
Saturdays, scraping moss off the stone lions' manes once
a week, and once a year a tournament at Darkrock Castle!
Nothing exciting ever happens here, Sisyphus. Never ever!'
Sighing, she sat down on the side of the bridge next to the
cat, and Sisyphus rubbed his grey head against her knee.

'I'm going to be twelve tomorrow, Sisyphus!' Igraine
went on. 'Twelve! And I haven't had a single real adventure.
How will I ever get to be a famous knight? Saving rabbits
from the fox, rescuing squirrels from pine martens?'

'No, saving fish from me,' purred Sisyphus, dipping his claws in the water, but this time his scaly prey got away from him.

Igraine looked up at the stone gargoyles. Some of them were yawning, and the rest were squinting crossly at the fat flies that liked to bask on their noses in the sun.

'I mean, look at that. Even the gargoyles are bored,' she said. 'I bet they'd like to crunch a few arrows or swallow a cannonball for a change.'

Sisyphus just shook his head, and went on staring patiently at the dark water.

'Yes, I know! It's silly to wish for that kind of thing.' Igraine jumped up so suddenly that the cat hissed at her angrily.

'You'll scare the fish away!'

'All you ever think about is food!' she snapped, reaching for the empty bucket. 'I'm going to die of boredom, you wait and see! Maybe not overnight, but definitely before my next birthday!'

Sisyphus dipped his paw into the water, and this time he threw a flapping fish up on to the bridge. 'Learn to work some magic!' he growled.

'I'm not interested in magic, you know that very well,' Igraine said. Gloomily she wandered back to the castle gate. 'Magic!' she muttered. 'Learning the ingredients for potions off by heart, magic spells, magic symbols, no thanks, not for me.'

'Pull the drawbridge up again!' mewed Sisyphus as he dragged his fish past her.

'What for?' she said. 'There's no one coming anyway. Twelve years old!' she murmured as she made for the armoury to the right of the gateway. 'My great-grandfather was a squire in a royal tournament when he was seven!' The door of the armoury was always well oiled, Igraine saw to that. Even if her parents didn't think much of weapons and armour (they thought their magic was much better protection) the armoury of Pimpernel Castle was still full of swords and suits of armour, shields and lances from the days of her great-grandfather Pelleas. He had been an enthusiastic knight but a terrible horseman, and never won a single tournament because he always fell off his horse before his opponent had so much as levelled his lance. Igraine often passed the time cleaning rust off his old swords, or polishing the shields that bore his coat of arms until they shone.

'I was born at the wrong time, that's all,' she muttered as she picked up one of his dented shields. 'Yes, that's what it is.' Her parents didn't like her to use the real swords, but very likely they'd be shut up in their workshop for some time yet, so Igraine chose a blade that looked fairly like the play-sword her father had made her by magic, stuck it in her belt and put a helmet with a crest like a silver bird on her head. Unfortunately it was too big for her, but it looked good all the same. Then she took the magical leather dummy off his stand. Albert and her parents had conjured him up for her eighth birthday.

When Igraine blew three times into the dummy's face, he stood upright, adjusted his sword belt, and stalked into the courtyard after her. Sisyphus put his ears back and hissed as the leathery creature marched out of the armoury.

'Oh, come on!' Igraine told him. 'You know he's not going to hurt you. And it's not as if I can practise fencing with you!' The leather man, limbs creaking, followed her up the stairs leading to the battlements above the castle gate. Sisyphus gloomily dropped a well-gnawed fishbone and leaped up the stairs after them.

While the cat made himself comfortable on the warm wall, the leather dummy leaned against the battlements, waiting. But Igraine clambered up on top of the wall and looked around. The sky was as blue as forget-me-nots. Only a few white clouds were drifting towards her from the Whispering Woods. It was such a clear day that if you looked west you could see all the way to the lands of the One-Eyed Duke, who was said to hunt dragons and unicorns all day, every day. The nearest village lay on one of the hills to the south. It was a long ride to get there, but on days like this you could see the cottage rooftops between the trees. To the east, however, the five round towers of Darkrock Castle rose to the sky. Darkrock was ten times bigger than Pimpernel, and its mistress the old

Baroness loved just two things in life: horses and honey beer.

'Nothing to do,' murmured Igraine. 'Nothing at all. This is really more than I can stand.' She leaned forward. 'Hello! Looks like the Baroness has a new banner. What coat of arms is that? Oh, well, it probably just shows a barrel of honey beer.' With a sigh, she jumped down from the wall and put the point of her sword to the leather dummy's chest.

'En garde, Leather Knight!' she cried, closing her visor. 'You sawed off my unicorn's horn, and you'll pay dearly for it!'

The leather man drew his sword and planted himself squarely in front of her. As usual, he parried her sword-strokes with the utmost elegance, and soon Igraine was so hot in her chain mail that she ran down to the well in the courtyard. She was just pouring a bucket of water over her head when the stone lions above the gate began to roar.

An Unexpected Visitor

The lions were roaring as hoarsely as if they had dust in their throats.

Startled, Igraine wiped the water out of her eyes, ran back up the steps to the battlements and pushed the leather man out of her way. Sisyphus stood on the wall, hissing. Igraine quickly knelt beside him and peered down.

The stone lions crouched on their ledge, teeth bared. Their tails were lashing the wall, and at the sound of their roars the startled water snakes put their heads out of the moat.

A horseman was galloping towards the castle from the east.

'What do you think you're doing?' Igraine shouted angrily at the lions. 'That's no stranger, you silly stone-faces. It's Bertram, Master of Horse at Darkrock Castle.'

'So it is!' growled the lion on the left, narrowing his eyes. 'She's right!'

'It's those doves,' the lion on the right defended himself.

'How can we keep a proper lookout with bird droppings in our eyes? Pretty soon I won't be able to tell a horse from a unicorn.'

'Yes, and the droppings stink to high heaven too!' growled the lion on the left. 'Doves have no respect these days.'

But Igraine wasn't listening any more. She ran down the steps with her mail-shirt clinking and raced across the courtyard. Sisyphus followed her at his leisure.

'Who's coming, my dear?' Sir Lamorak called from the tower window.

'Oh, just a false alarm from the lions again,' Igraine called back. 'It's Bertram, Master of Horse from Darkrock.'

'Oh, no!' groaned her father. 'That can only mean one thing – the Baroness wants to hold one of her boring horse-race meetings. Tell her we can't come, my angel, all right?'

Then he disappeared again – before Igraine could remind him that she personally didn't think horse races were in the least boring.

Bertram the Master of Horse rode into the castle at the gallop. His face was as red as her parents' magic cloaks, and his horse was snorting and sweating. Igraine quickly fetched a bucket of water and rubbed the horse down with a handful of straw, while its exhausted master slipped out of the saddle.

'What weather!' panted Bertram. 'I'd sooner have torrents of rain. Where's your father, Igraine?'

'Casting spells to make my birthday present,' said Igraine, stroking the horse's mane back from its forehead. 'And you'd better not disturb him. Is the Baroness going to hold some horse races?'

Bertram shook his head. 'No,' he said. 'I'm afraid the news I bring is nothing like that. Call your parents, Igraine, even if it does mean that your birthday present has to wait.'

BAD NEWS

'**W**hat is it, Bertram?' asked the Fair Melisande as she and Sir Lamorak entered the Great Hall.

Of course Albert had come with them, even though Igraine had sent Sisyphus to tell him that he at least was to carry on working on her present. His hair was covered with silvery powder, and Igraine's parents didn't look much tidier, but all the same the Master of Horse bowed deeply to the Fair Melisande.

'Distressing news, Your Loveliness,' he said.

Igraine's father raised his eyebrows. 'Oh, no! Don't say the old Baroness has . . .'

'No, no.' Bertram looked all round, as if the paintings on the walls might hear him. 'No, she's all right, but a few days ago she had an unwelcome visit from her nephew Osmund, the one who turned out so badly. Osmund the Greedy, everyone calls him. And he came with his castellan, who never opens his visor except to eat.'

'Oh, a knight?' Igraine was sitting on the long table where her great-grandfather Pelleas had carved his initials. 'What sort of armour does he wear?'

'It has spikes all over it, from his helmet to the greaves on his legs,' said Bertram. 'A nasty piece of work, just like the man inside it. Yesterday morning,' he went on, lowering his voice, 'just when I was getting the horses fed, Osmund suddenly announces at the crack of dawn that the Baroness has gone on pilgrimage and won't be back for a year at the earliest. And guess what: he claims she's left him in charge of Darkrock and all her lands while she's away.'

'The Baroness on pilgrimage?' Sir Lamorak frowned. 'But she never leaves her room except to see that her horses are all right.'

'Or to drink honey beer,' said Igraine.

'Exactly!' Bertram nodded. 'No one saw her leave, and she didn't go to the stables either. Do you think she'd have gone away without saying goodbye to her favourite horse Lancelot? Ask your daughter! She's visited the Baroness often enough.'

Igraine wiped some dove droppings off her mail-shirt. 'Impossible,' she said. 'The Baroness never even went to bed without visiting Lancelot first. And she poured a little honey beer in his water before breakfast every morning – even though I kept telling her that honey beer would do him no good at all.'

Albert frowned, which he could do quite impressively, and Igraine's parents exchanged anxious glances.

'That certainly does sound peculiar, Bertram,' said Melisande. 'What do you suggest we should do? Shall we go back to Darkrock with you? Shall we ask this Osmund to tell us exactly where his aunt went?'

But Darkrock's Master of Horse firmly shook his head. 'No, no, Your Loveliness! I haven't come to ask you for help. I'm here to warn you. I think Osmund is a threat to your castle and your family.'

'A threat to us? How?' asked Albert, removing a mouse from his hair.

'It's my belief . . .' Bertram looked around him again, as if fearing he'd be overheard. 'It's my belief this man Osmund

came to Darkrock only to mount an attack on Pimpernel.'

'Indeed?' Sir Lamorak raised his eyebrows. 'Well, well. I expect you have some reason for that suspicion?'

'He wants your Books of Magic, sire! His servants talk of nothing else. He's planning to use your books to make himself the greatest magician in the world. And I assure you, when Osmund wants something he takes it. Not for nothing is he known as Osmund the Greedy.'

'Yes, I think I've heard a few stories about him and his castellan with the spiky armour,' murmured Sir Lamorak. 'Not very nice stories. But his aunt the Baroness is such a charming old lady. Even if she does like honey beer a little too much.'

'Osmund is stirring up feeling against you, sir!' Bertram went on. 'He's spreading word that you don't deserve to own such powerful books if all you do with them is make trees blossom in winter and conjure up magical presents for your children!'

'Ah. I see,' murmured Sir Lamorak. A little silver powder fell on his shoes as he ran his fingers through his hair.

'Osmund's castellan is offering the villagers bags full of gold to tell him about the defences of your castle,' said Bertram. 'And that spiky brute puts his sword to the throats of those who don't take his gold and keep their mouths shut. He wants to know everything – whether the stone lions can do anything apart from roaring, how dangerous the snakes in the castle moat are, whether the gargoyles can really devour arrows and spit fire.' Bertram looked at Sir Lamorak with concern. 'The people of the village like you, sir. You're kind and generous, you've helped almost all of them at some time or other. But Osmund's castellan knows how to frighten them!'

'Those poor people,' said Melisande angrily. 'Bertram, next time you're in the village, would you be good enough to tell everyone they're welcome to pass on all they know to that castellan? What can he discover that's so important, anyway? And if this man Osmund really does attack us, then Lamorak and I will think up a few nice little magic surprises for him, won't we, my love?'

'Definitely,' said Sir Lamorak.

'He will attack, Your Loveliness!' said Bertram, his voice husky with concern. 'More soldiers are coming to Darkrock every day; heaven knows where Osmund finds them all. They're streaming into the castle from all points of the compass, and his spiky castellan is bringing in horses, arms and armour. As you know, the Baroness stored nothing but her barrels of beer in the prison tower, but Osmund is having the place fitted out as a dungeon again, and I'm afraid you're meant to be his next guests in it.' Bertram shook his head. 'Yes, I fear he's going to come calling at Pimpernel Castle very soon, and it won't be a friendly visit.'

'Ah, well!' Sir Lamorak sighed, and his eyes wandered over the portraits of his ancestors. 'Pimpernel has had unwelcome visitors many times before, and all of them wanted the Books of Magic. But the books are still here. No, I'm not worried. The Baroness's disappearance is a far worse headache. As soon as Igraine's birthday is over I'll ride to Darkrock and find out whether our old friend has really gone on pilgrimage. But thank you very much for telling us all this, Bertram. Will you stay to dinner? Good heavens, I believe we haven't even had breakfast yet!'

'Thank you very much, sir,' said Bertram, bowing to Igraine's parents and then to her and Albert, 'but I must get back before anyone notices my absence. Do be careful, and please take my warning seriously!' Then he turned and walked to the door with a heavy tread.

'Wait a minute, Bertram!' cried Igraine, following him into the courtyard.

'Pull the drawbridge up the moment I've left, Igraine,' Bertram told her. 'Bar the gates, and keep well away from Darkrock while Osmund is lording it there! No fencing practice with the servants, no secret rides on Lancelot! And I'm afraid you and I won't be able to meet for some time.'

Igraine didn't answer. She looked out of the gateway and to the east, to the place where the strange banner flew from the towers of Darkrock Castle.

'Don't you think it might be useful for someone to spy on that Osmund?' she said. 'I mean, he wouldn't know who I am!'

'Don't you dare!' Bertram picked up his reins. 'I will personally throw you into the moat if I catch you at Darkrock. And I'll never take you to a tournament like I promised! I've told you all there is to know about Darkrock at the moment, so enjoy your birthday, and pray for Osmund to die of indigestion before he can stretch his greedy fingers out to Pimpernel. Oh, yes,' he added, putting his hand into his saddlebag and bringing out a beautiful bridle, 'and this is for your pony. A little present from me and the grooms so that you'll remember us when you're a famous knight. I know it's supposed to be unlucky to give presents before someone's birthday, but who knows when we'll see each other again?'

'Oh, thank you, Bertram!' gasped Igraine, stroking the soft leather.

'See you some time!' called the Master of Horse as he rode over the bridge and away. Back to Darkrock.

A Little Magic Mistake

By that evening everyone at Pimpernel had forgotten about Bertram's bad news. Igraine's parents were still casting spells, but now rainbow-coloured smoke was drifting out of the tower window, which always meant that they'd nearly finished. When dusk fell Igraine couldn't stand it any more. Once again she climbed the stairs to the tower, but just as she was standing at its heavy oak door the visor of her helmet snapped shut, and Albert chased her right through the castle and into her room. Then he cast a spell to lock the door, and set off back to the magic workshop, whistling. Of course, Igraine tried climbing out of the window the minute he'd gone, but as soon as she put a foot on the windowsill six fat, bright-green spiders started spinning a web in front of her nose. Albert knew very well what scared his little sister. So Igraine could only wait for her birthday to come.

At last, when the moon was shining in the sky above the

castle tower, she took off her mail-shirt and lay down on the bed. Sisyphus snuggled up beside her and soon began snoring with his head on her stomach (he snored almost like a human being). But Igraine lay awake listening to the strange songs that the night wind blew over from the tower, wondering about her present. Then she remembered Bertram's anxious face. She tried to imagine what Osmund looked like and his castellan too, the knight with iron spikes all over his armour, but she didn't make a very good job of it. Perhaps adventure has finally come to Pimpernel, she thought, but she wasn't so sure that she still liked the idea. Sisyphus woke with a start when she turned over restlessly, and hissed at her. Would the Baroness really go on pilgrimage without saying goodbye to Lancelot? she wondered. Then she finally fell asleep.

It was the middle of the night when she was woken by someone hammering on her door. In alarm, she sat up and saw Albert standing in the doorway with a lantern in his hand.

'What's up?' she asked sleepily, pushing Sisyphus off her legs.

Albert cleared his throat in embarrassment, and brushed pink icing sugar out of his untidy hair.

'Er, well, it's like this,' he stammered, clearing his throat again. 'We've had a little magic mistake, a slip of the tongue, these things happen sometimes, you see . . .'

Igraine jumped out of bed and went to the window.

But the castle courtyard lay quiet and peaceful in the moonlight, and the tower wasn't leaning any further sideways than usual.

'What kind of mistake?' she asked, turning suspiciously to Albert. 'Has my birthday present gone up in rainbow-coloured smoke?'

'Oh, no. Nothing like that,' Albert made haste to reply. 'Your present is ready. It – er – it looks wonderful, only . . . only . . .' he ran his hands through his hair again, 'only just as we were going to add the finishing touch, Mother made a slip of the tongue, and it happened.'

'What?' cried Igraine. 'What happened?'

'You'll see in a moment.' Without another word, Albert took her hand and led her through the dark castle, over the moonlit courtyard, across the narrow bridge and up the staircase to the tower, until they stood in front of the workshop door. Downcast, Albert pushed it open.

The Books of Magic were running about in great agitation, waving their arms and muttering to themselves. And among the jars full of leaves, flowers and ground

minerals stood two pigs. One black and one pink.

'Hello, honey,' said the black pig, in the Fair Melisande's beautiful voice.

'We're in a bit of a fix, what?' said the pink pig in Sir Lamorak's unmistakable voice.

Igraine gasped for air, opened her eyes so wide that they almost popped out of her head – and found that she couldn't utter a sound.

'Luckily we'd as good as finished your present. There was just one little detail to be added,' said her father – or rather, the pig with her father's voice. 'Oh, do please keep still, books!'

The Books of Magic, their feelings injured, sat down on the carpet.

'There it is, honey,' said the black pig, trotting over to a huge parcel lying on Sir Lamorak's magic armchair. 'Albert stopped to wrap it up before he went to wake you. Would you like to open it now or wait till after breakfast?'

Igraine looked first at the huge parcel and then at her bristly, curly-tailed mother. 'I think I'd rather open it when you've changed yourselves back again,' she said.

The Books of Magic broke into mocking laughter.

'Er, well, my dear,' grunted Sir Lamorak, scratching his snout rather clumsily with one back trotter, 'there's a tiny little problem there. I'm afraid we found out that the jar of giant's red hairs is empty.'

'Completely empty,' added the Fair Melisande, sighing.

'So what does that mean?' asked Igraine uneasily. She could never remember just what all the magic ingredients were for.

'We told Albert that jar was empty two months ago,' complained a fat book with a gilded cover. 'But he's so careless. He'll never get to be a good magician that way.'

The other books nudged each other and nodded, sneering.

'Yes, all right, I know. I ought to have gone to find more at once!' Albert gave the books a nasty glance. 'But giant's hairs don't exactly grow beside every castle moat, do they?'

'So what exactly does all of this mean?' cried Igraine impatiently.

Her brother cleared his throat. 'Without the giant's

hairs,' he said, 'our parents will stay pigs.'

'No doubt about it,' croaked the smallest book. 'Nothing to be done. All over. Finished.'

'What?' cried Igraine, horrified. 'Are you saying I have a couple of pigs for parents from now on?'

'It's not all that unpleasant being a pig, honey,' said Melisande, who still had beautiful blue eyes. 'So if you don't mind very much . . .'

'Well, not very much,' murmured Igraine, looking down at her parents. Suddenly she just had to smile. 'You do look funny,' she said. 'Especially you, Papa. But pink suits you.'

'How kind!' said Sir Lamorak shyly, rubbing his nose against a chair leg.

'Couldn't I find some giant's hairs somewhere?' asked Igraine. 'Where did you get them from before?'

'Oh, there are several giants in these parts,' replied her father. 'But it would mean a long ride for you, and these are wild and dangerous times.'

'Who cares?' Igraine shrugged her shoulders. 'I've often found you magic ingredients before. I like doing it.'

'Let's discuss it later,' said the Fair Melisande. 'I think we all need some sleep now. You too, books. Off you go, back on the shelves.'

Grumbling, the Books of Magic scrambled up and climbed the narrow ladders to their bookshelves, where they leaned against each other, closed their eyes and were all snoring fit to bust in a moment. Casting spells is strenuous work, even for Books of Magic.

'What do you think, Lamorak?' whispered Melisande. 'Would we be more comfortable in the stables or downstairs in front of the hearth?'

'I'd prefer the stables,' replied Sir Lamorak quietly, and yawned, which looks rather odd in a pig.

So Albert and Igraine took their parents to the stables, made them a comfortable bed of clean straw, and then left them alone – with the horses, who looked disapproving when they saw their new companions, and foolish when the pigs began talking in their owners' voices.

BIRTHDAY BREAKFAST ON THE CARPET

When Igraine opened her eyes on her twelfth birthday, Sisyphus was sitting on her stomach. He mewed, 'Many happy returns!' and deposited a dead fish on her forehead.

'Oh, thank you, Sisyphus!' she murmured sleepily, although she thought his present was rather nasty.

'Don't mention it,' purred the tomcat. 'Breakfast in the magic workshop.' Then he padded away.

'I'll soon know what my present is!' murmured Igraine. 'Soon, soon, soon!' And she was so excited that she could hardly do up the buttons of her silly dress. She always wore a dress on birthdays, in honour of the day and because her father liked making magic dresses for her. Her father! For a moment Igraine had quite forgotten that her parents had curly tails now. I'll go and get those giant's hairs tomorrow, she thought, yes, that's what I'll do. But now she just had to see her present. What luck it hadn't turned into a pig too!

Birthday breakfasts were always in the workshop, because the Books of Magic liked to watch presents being unwrapped.

'Happy birthday, Igraine, happy birthday to you!' they all chanted as she opened the door. Igraine was fond of the books, though they thought rather too highly of their magic powers and insisted on being dusted every Wednesday and Saturday. They really could work wonderful magic if an experienced magician used them; one who had the necessary ingredients, could decipher the mysterious writing on their pages and had passed at least Grade Seven of the magic exams. It was said that almost a hundred years ago two of Igraine's great-great-uncles had exploded when they tried using the books after passing only Grade Three!

Albert was wearing his golden magic coat, as he always did on special occasions, and he had cast a spell to give his mice red spots on their grey fur. Sisyphus looked hungrily at them, but of course he wouldn't touch so much as the tip of a tail for fear of Albert. Igraine's parents wore necklaces of sugar hearts around their piggy necks, and the books sat on their shelves, threw confetti down on Igraine, and sang in high voices:

'Happy birthday, dear Igraine.
Waiting was a dreadful pain.
Everything today's for you,
Birthday cake and presents too.'

44

'Oh, thank you!' cried Igraine. 'Thank you, books!'

A wonderful birthday breakfast was laid out on the carpet, with a birthday cake, pancakes, waffles, scrambled eggs, and cat biscuits for Sisyphus.

'I'm sorry, my dear,' said Sir Lamorak, trotting over to his daughter on his pink piggy legs. 'Pigs aren't good at sitting on chairs. Your mother and I tried it this morning, and it just doesn't work. So I'm afraid we must have your birthday breakfast on the carpet this year.'

'Oh, I like it there,' said Igraine, kneeling down on the floor.

Albert bowed to her and put a big parcel into her arms. 'Here you are, sister dear. From Father, Mother, me and the Singing Books.'

The parcel weighed very little for its size, and the red wrapping paper smelled of roses when she undid it. Her parents poked their snouts expectantly over her shoulders, and the Books of Magic leaned so far forward that one of them fell off its shelf and landed in the cat biscuits.

Inside the parcel there was a suit of armour – a wonderful, shimmering silver suit of armour, with a helmet that had a white bird spreading its wings on the crest. Its long tail was made of peacock feathers, and when Igraine carefully put the helmet on she was amazed to find that it was hardly any heavier than the plumed tail itself. The whole suit of armour weighed so little that it seemed to be made of nothing but light and air. And when

Igraine climbed cautiously into it, the metal fitted her like a second skin.

'Well, do you like it?' asked her mother, who still had a few blades of straw stuck among her bristles from her night in the stables.

'Oh, it's wonderful!' breathed Igraine. 'Truly, truly, truly wonderful.'

The Books of Magic chuckled and applauded each other.

'And it will grow with you,' said Sir Lamorak, scratching his ear with his back trotter. He did it very elegantly now, although he'd been a pig for just one night.

'That's right,' said Albert happily. 'We cast spells so that it will still fit you if you ever get to be tall and fat.'

Igraine stroked the shining suit and smiled.

'And nothing can get through it,' said her father proudly. 'Nothing at all. Even lances will bounce back from this armour. It's supposed to be waterproof too . . . at least, the books say so.'

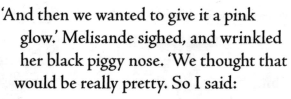

'And then we wanted to give it a pink glow.' Melisande sighed, and wrinkled her black piggy nose. 'We thought that would be really pretty. So I said:

"Silver be this armour fine,
With a pink and rosy . . ."'

'. . . *swine,*' said Albert. 'Mama went and said "swine" instead of "shine". And then it happened. Father turned into a pink pig. But why Mother turned into a pig too, and a black one at that, while nothing happened to me, is more than we can explain.'

'That's magic for you,' said Igraine, striding up and down in her birthday present. Nothing about it clinked, nothing squeaked. Magic did have its advantages. 'I'll wear it tomorrow when I ride off to find the giant,' she said. 'Or do you think I'd better set out today?'

'No, no!' cried her parents. 'Definitely not. Today we're celebrating your birthday.'

'And anyway,' added Sir Lamorak, 'your mother and I are still wondering whether it isn't too dangerous a task for you. Perhaps we ought to go ourselves.'

'Nonsense,' said Igraine. 'Running around in the wilderness is much more dangerous for pigs. Someone might catch and eat you! No, I'm going, and that's that. Which giant should I ask for some of his hairs? As far as I know there's one in the hills in the west, and another who lives beyond the Whispering Woods.'

'Garleff is the friendliest, he's the giant in the west,' replied Sir Lamorak, trying to get his pink snout into the milk jug. 'The giant beyond the forest is too fond of catching humans and giving them to his children to play with. Anyway, his hair is more brown than red.'

'Yes, if you do go, ride to Garleff,' agreed the Fair Melisande. 'Your father charmed away a nasty rash he had a few years ago. Giants don't forget that kind of thing, not for ages. They're very grateful creatures.'

'What about me?' Albert passed his curly-tailed parents the birthday cake. He sounded rather injured. 'I'm older than Igraine, and I'm a considerably better magician. Why can't I go and get the hairs?'

Igraine was greatly tempted to stick her tongue out at him.

'Because your sister rides considerably better than you do,' replied the Fair Melisande. 'I'm afraid you take after your great-grandfather Pelleas. And as we all know, he always fell off his horse at the wrong time.'

'And in addition to that,' said Sir Lamorak, smacking his lips – obviously the cake tasted good to pigs as well as people – 'in addition to that, my boy, we may need your magic arts here in the near future.'

Albert looked at his father in surprise. 'Why?'

'For the same reason that forces us to let Igraine go on this mission alone,' replied Sir Lamorak. 'I confess that under these slightly changed circumstances the news our dear friend Bertram brought make me a little anxious. Suppose this Osmund really does turn up here soon? To be sure, Pimpernel Castle can defend itself. The lions will roar, the gargoyles will swallow any missiles. And the magic of the moat will certainly work too. None of that, however, will be enough if Osmund attacks the castle with a large army.'

'But you can simply magic the army away!' cried Albert. 'You can turn all the soldiers into ants or woodlice if you want to.'

The two pigs exchanged gloomy glances.

'I'm afraid it's not that simple,' said Sir Lamorak. 'Your mother and I have found out that now we're pigs we can't work magic at all.'

'What?' Now it was Igraine and Albert who looked anxious.

'Not the least little scrap of magic,' said the Fair Melisande. 'That's why we need those giant's hairs as soon as possible, and you, Albert, will have to defend the castle until we can cast spells again.'

Up on their shelves, the Singing Books groaned.

'Luckily we'd made the birthday breakfast in advance, or else . . .' Sir Lamorak fell silent, but Igraine ended his sentence for him.

'Or else breakfast would have been blue eggs and dry biscuits this morning.'

Albert went as red as a beetroot. 'All right, all right, little sister, I'm working on it!'

'You'd better,' said Igraine, standing up. 'But anyway, that settles one thing. I must set off today. In fact, at once.'

'No, no, no!' grunted her father, shaking his pink ears energetically. 'Out of the question. We're celebrating your birthday today. Tomorrow's soon enough to decide whether you really do go to find the giant. I still don't like the idea. You'd most likely be back within four days on your pony, but then again it probably wouldn't take your mother and me more than a week. At least, so I assume,' he added, looking doubtfully at his pink trotters. 'I don't have the faintest idea how good pigs are at hiking. But in any case, it would be the devil's own luck if Osmund arrived with his men before we're rid of our curly tails.'

Sometimes, however, the devil does have all the luck. Then it's just one thing after another. And troubles seldom come alone.

OSMUND
THE GREEDY

Osmund came the very next morning.
Mist still hung over the meadows, and Igraine
was saddling her pony while Sisyphus rubbed
uneasily around her legs. Albert was sitting astride one of
the stone lions, cleaning dove droppings out of its eyes. He
almost fell off its back when it roared in alarm.

'Oh, hang it!' he said angrily. 'Are you up to your old
tricks again? There's no excuse this time!'

Igraine raced up the flight of steps as fast as she could,
but Sisyphus slipped between her legs and was up on the
wall first.

'Albert, get off that lion!' called Igraine once she had
looked over the battlements, but her brother was already
hiding behind them.

Horsemen emerged from the mist in the east.
Horsemen in grey armour. They were riding towards
Pimpernel Castle.

'Sisyphus, go and fetch our parents!' Igraine whispered.

'Quick! They're still in the stables.'

Sisyphus shot away as if a pack of wolves were after him.

'What do you bet it's our new neighbour, little sister?' asked Albert in a low voice.

Igraine didn't answer.

For where but Darkrock could the horsemen be coming from? There were a great many of them, so many that Igraine soon lost count. A fat man in a black cloak rode at the head of the troop, with a gigantic knight following him. The strange banner that Igraine had seen flying from the towers of Darkrock was fluttering from his lance.

'A visit from the neighbours?' Igraine's father was badly out of breath after climbing the steep steps to the battlements on his piggy legs.

'Goodness me, this looks like trouble, my dear,' said Melisande, pushing her snout above the wall. Sisyphus jumped up on the battlements, his tail raised high, and hissed at the visitors below.

The horsemen were coming closer and closer. The cold morning air was filled with the clanking of their weapons and armour. They were hardly a horse's length from the castle moat when their stout leader reined in his mount and raised his gloved hand. His men swarmed forward, taking their horses up to the moat until they surrounded it like a wall, leaving only a space in front of the drawbridge for their master and the knight with the lance. The knight's armour looked exactly as Bertram had described

it; it was covered from his neck to his greaves with iron spikes. Even his helmet was as prickly as a sweet chestnut husk.

When Osmund (for who else could the leader be?) took up his position in front of the drawbridge, the Spiky Knight followed, and planted his lance on the ground between himself and his master.

The lions were still roaring, but when Albert snapped his fingers they stopped.

'Hide!' Igraine whispered urgently to the two pigs. Her parents hesitated, but finally stuck their heads under Albert's magic coat. Meanwhile Igraine climbed up on the battlements. Luckily she'd put on her new armour when she got up that morning.

'Who are you?' she called down as loudly as she could. 'And what do you want?'

The Spiky Knight opened his visor and looked up at her. His face was white as snow.

'I am the castellan of Osmund the Magnificent!' he called across the marshy water. 'Osmund is the new master of Darkrock Castle, and he presents his compliments to his neighbours at Pimpernel.'

'How kind!' Igraine called down. 'Same to him. And now you can all ride home again.'

'Hush, Igraine!' hissed Albert. 'Let's hear what they have to say.'

Igraine pressed her lips together and kept quiet, hard as that was.

The horses were snorting uneasily. They could scent the water snakes. But the Spiky Knight forced his own mount closer to the moat.

'The noble Osmund didn't come to bandy words with children!' he called up to Igraine. 'Especially not with an impertinent minx like you. Take a look at that!' he told his men. 'Here's a castle where they put little girls in armour. They really scare us, don't they?'

The horsemen gave such a loud roar of laughter that the water snakes lifted their heads out of the water. Whinnying, the horses reared. Five men fell head first into the moat and disappeared beneath the water lilies. The Spiky Knight angrily signalled to his men to pull them out, but however hard they looked their companions had disappeared, armour, swords, pennants and all.

'The moat magic still works all right!' whispered Albert.

'That's good news!' the Fair Melisande whispered back. 'The sheer nastiness of this Osmund and his castellan is getting up my nose like the stink of sulphur!'

'Hey, you down there, you can save yourselves the trouble of searching!' Igraine put her hands on her hips. 'Anyone who falls into our moat turns into a fish. But don't worry, I've already fed the water snakes today.'

Osmund's men were getting restless. But when their master cast a menacing glance all around, they fell perfectly silent again.

'That's enough silly children's talk!' cried Osmund. His voice sounded like the growling of a fat tomcat, and his black cloak billowed out in the wind. 'Where are the enchantress Melisande and her husband Lamorak? Is this your idea of hospitality, turning brave men into fish?'

'Talks big, doesn't he?' murmured Albert. 'I don't think I like him one little bit.'

'Can't you turn him into a woodlouse or a fat frog?' whispered Igraine, without taking her eyes off Osmund.

'Answer the noble Osmund, you little toad in armour!'
bellowed the Spiky Knight. 'Where are your parents, the
enchanters Melisande and Lamorak?'

'Not at home!' Igraine shouted back. 'But you can
always come back next week and try again.'

Osmund obviously didn't care for this information at
all. 'Listen to me, little girl!' he called menacingly back. 'I
don't care where your parents are. Tell them that I want
their Singing Books of Magic! I'm ready to pay whatever
you and your skinny beanpole of a brother weigh in gold.
But if they turn down this extremely generous offer,' he
added, drawing his sword and laying it across his knees,
'I'll be back with an army, to tear down this miserable
castle stone by stone. And no magic in the world will
prevent me from taking the books by force. Will you tell
them that?'

Igraine started trembling with rage.

'I want an answer by noon tomorrow!' cried Osmund. 'I
shall send my castellan to hear it as soon as the sun stands
above that ridiculously wonky castle tower of yours.'

'You can have your answer now, you puffed-up toad!'
Igraine shouted down. 'You—'

But she got no further. Albert grabbed her from behind,
put his hand over her mouth and pulled her down from
the wall. 'Are you crazy?' he hissed in her ear. 'Have
you forgotten that our parents can't work magic at the
moment? And it isn't as easy as you think to turn them

all into woodlice! We have to play for time. Only that can save us!'

He let go of Igraine and climbed up on the battlements himself. His magic coat fluttered around his tall, thin figure, and the mice hid in his sleeves.

'Forgive my little sister, noble Osmund!' cried Albert, bowing low. 'She's only just twelve, and she's heard minstrels tell too many tales of chivalry. I am Albert of Pimpernel, eldest son of noble Sir Lamorak and the Fair Melisande. I will inform my parents of your generous offer as soon as they get back from their journey. But we're not expecting them for another two weeks. So I must ask you not to expect an answer any sooner than that.'

Igraine could almost have bitten off her tongue with fury when she heard her brother talk like that. But Albert was right. They needed time – time to go and get the giant's hairs. Time to turn their parents back into human form. Otherwise they were finished.

'Oh, I could bite my curly tail with rage!' grunted her father beside her. 'Why does that fellow have to show up just now? I'd turn him straight into a slug if I wasn't stuck in this stupid itchy pigskin, I'd turn him into a stinkhorn, I'd turn him into the backside of an ape . . .'

'Sssh!' hissed the Fair Melisande, listening with bated breath for an answer from below.

None came for an agonizingly long time. Then they heard Osmund's voice again. 'Oho! So your parents have gone away, have they? For two weeks. Leaving their children all alone in a crumbling castle like this for two whole weeks?' Some of his men laughed. 'Hm. All alone with their lovely Books of Magic. Well, well. Two weeks, that's really quite a while. But I'll wait for the answer, my boy. After all, I'm a man of honour, aren't I?'

Igraine clenched her fists with fury. But Osmund smiled mockingly at his castellan.

The Spiky Knight raised his lance, and Osmund's men turned their horses and rode away with their master. Only the Spiky Knight lingered by the castle moat for another moment, motionless. He looked up at the walls, examined the gargoyles, the drawbridge and the leaning tower that rose above the battlements. Then he bent forward, spat into the moat where the water snakes were writhing, swung his horse round and galloped away.

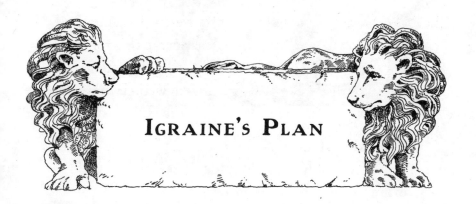

IGRAINE'S PLAN

'**N**ow what? You can bet Osmund won't wait two weeks to come back,' said Albert.

He and Igraine were sitting side by side on the carpet in the magic workshop. The Singing Books were sitting on their shelves, looking depressed, and Sir Lamorak and the Fair Melisande were trotting restlessly about among their items of magic equipment.

'No, he certainly won't,' sighed Melisande. 'In fact he'll be back very soon, because he thinks it's going to be easy for him.'

'And he's probably right,' said Albert gloomily. 'Perhaps we ought to take the books and all hide in the Whispering Wood, before he throws me and Igraine into Darkrock's dungeon and turns you two into roast pork.'

'No, no, we most definitely ought not!' cried Sir Lamorak, stamping his trotter. 'We're not done for yet. You're already a good magician, Albert, and the books can help you.'

A worried muttering was heard up on the shelves.
'But he's only passed Grade Three of the magic
exams!' said one of the fatter books.

'That's right!' agreed a very slim volume. 'We can't
possibly work with such a beginner. He doesn't even
know how to read our writing properly.'

Albert jumped up. 'Of course I do!' he said in
an injured tone. 'And I know the page numbers of
almost all your magic songs. Even my mice practically
know them by heart, I've said those numbers out
loud to myself so often!'

'But that . . . that . . . !' The books were
whispering to each other. 'That's an insult!' one of
them squawked.

'Oh, don't make such a fuss!' said Igraine,
taking her brother's side. 'We're good
enough to dust you, right? But when it
comes to working
magic . . .'

'Hush, hush,
hush, my
dears!'

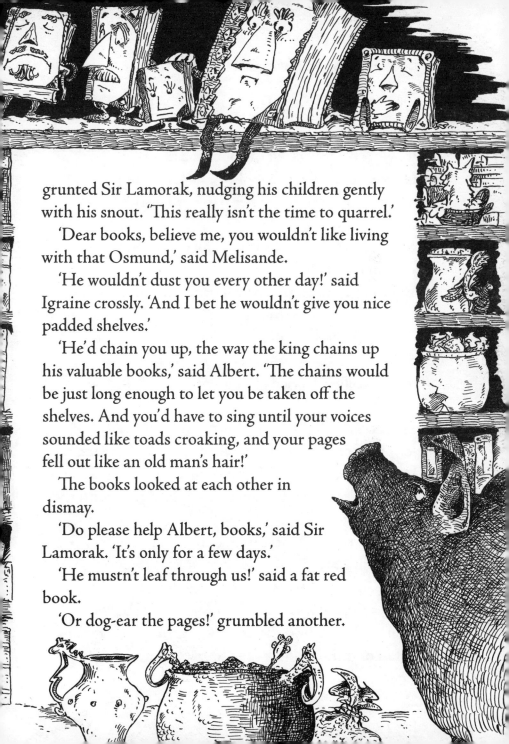

grunted Sir Lamorak, nudging his children gently with his snout. 'This really isn't the time to quarrel.'

'Dear books, believe me, you wouldn't like living with that Osmund,' said Melisande.

'He wouldn't dust you every other day!' said Igraine crossly. 'And I bet he wouldn't give you nice padded shelves.'

'He'd chain you up, the way the king chains up his valuable books,' said Albert. 'The chains would be just long enough to let you be taken off the shelves. And you'd have to sing until your voices sounded like toads croaking, and your pages fell out like an old man's hair!'

The books looked at each other in dismay.

'Do please help Albert, books,' said Sir Lamorak. 'It's only for a few days.'

'He mustn't leaf through us!' said a fat red book.

'Or dog-ear the pages!' grumbled another.

'No bookmarks, and always a civil tone of voice, if you please.'

'All right, all right!' muttered Albert. 'I'm not a beginner, you know!'

'Oh, yes, you are!' cried the books. Then they put their heads together and whispered, while Albert juggled his mice and Igraine scratched her parents' bristles (pigs' backs tend to get very itchy).

At last one of the books tipped forward and leaned down from the shelf to them.

'Very well,' it muttered. 'We'll help Albert. Just for once, and only on account of the adverse and extremely ominous circumstances. What's more, we don't think that man Osmund is worthy to be our new master.'

'Good, excellent!' cried Sir Lamorak. 'In that case . . .'

'In that case I'm riding off this minute to find those giant's hairs,' said Igraine.

Her piggy parents immediately drooped their ears.

'Don't look so sad,' said Igraine, putting her arms round their bristly necks. 'I'll be back in two days' time with the hairs, you wait and see.'

'Two days' time?' Albert wrinkled his sharp nose in derision. 'How are you planning to do that? Have you learned to fly now, little sister?'

'No, but I'm going to take the fastest horse between the Whispering Wood and the Giant's Hills,' replied Igraine. 'You'd fall off him the first time he broke into a gallop.'

'What are you talking about, honey?' asked her mother, sounding worried.

'I can't go on my pony, Mama,' said Igraine. 'That would take at least four days, and Osmund will be here very soon, you said so yourselves. I wouldn't be any faster on one of our other horses, either. They're all dear creatures, but slow and a bit too stout. And as for Albert's powers as a magician, no offence intended, but the books are right: he is still a beginner, so I'd better be as quick as I can.'

'Meaning what?' said Albert. 'You want me to conjure you up some wings?'

'No,' said Igraine, 'they'd probably fall off while I was still flying over the moat. Meaning I'm going to borrow Lancelot. On him I can do the journey in two days, not four.'

'The Baroness's favourite horse Lancelot?' Albert looked at Igraine as if she was out of her mind. 'That horse is so wild that no one can ride him!'

'Well, I . . .' Igraine avoided looking at her parents. 'I've often ridden him before.'

'You've done what?' cried the horrified Sir Lamorak.

'Every time I went to see Bertram,' muttered Igraine. 'He didn't want to let me at first, but when he saw how well Lancelot and I get on he said no more. And the Baroness never noticed a thing, because I only rode him while she was sitting in her room drinking honey beer.'

'But you can't go to Darkrock, not now!' cried Albert.

'The place is teeming with soldiers. And suppose you run into Osmund or his spiky castellan? Have you forgotten that they've both seen you before?'

'Oh, no, they haven't,' said Igraine. 'They saw my armour, that's all.' She took off her helmet and shook out her hair, which was as black as her mother's. 'I'll put a dress on and ride to Darkrock on our donkey – taking my suit of armour with me, of course. Then I'll go to the stables, get Bertram to bring me Lancelot, and I'll be off again right away.'

Sir Lamorak shook his head, looking anxious. 'I really don't like it, my dear,' he said. 'I definitely don't. It sounds very, very risky.'

'Nonsense!' cried Igraine, stripping off her wonderful armour. 'It's nothing for me, Papa. Really and truly. Word of knightly honour.' Then she kissed her parents on their snouts, made a face at Albert, and went to the door.

'She won't be back!' moaned the books as she left. 'The giant will tread on her. Or the Spiky Knight will skewer her – and we'll have to work magic with Albert until our glue wears out! That's what will happen.'

But Igraine wasn't listening. She was already on her way down the tower stairs.

At Darkrock Castle

Everything had changed at Darkrock Castle. When Igraine last visited, the old Baroness's cats had been basking in the sun on the battlements, and she had stumbled over chickens running about in the courtyard between the outer walls and the main keep. Now the battlements were swarming with guards, and knights were crowding outside the gate. The clink of weapons could be heard beyond the high walls, and wooden carts full of hay were coming up the narrow road from the village to feed the horses of Osmund's army.

The guards at the gate, swords at the ready, checked everyone who wanted to go into the castle. But when a girl of twelve rode up on a rather stout donkey, carrying a basket of new-laid eggs, they let her pass without any trouble. So Igraine entered Osmund's castle.

She had hidden her armour and her sword in the bundle of clothes hanging over the donkey's back, and the basket of eggs she was using as camouflage contained one that Albert had enchanted. As soon as she was past the guards she cracked it on the castle wall, and out slipped a tiny grey bird. It would fly away and warn Albert the moment Osmund and his army set off for Pimpernel.

Igraine watched the little spy flutter up to the highest of the castle turrets. Then she rode her donkey through the crowd of people in the castle courtyard, making for the stables. Bertram was sure to be there at this time of day. She took the donkey to the stables where the Baroness's ponies were kept, near the clock tower. There were several donkeys there too, and no one would notice that another had suddenly joined them. Lancelot's stable stood opposite. Sweating grooms were shovelling muck out of the boxes, but Lancelot's box had already been cleared. The stallion looked bored; he was nibbling the wood of his manger and prancing restlessly from leg to leg. Igraine opened the door of his box and slipped in.

'Hello, Lancelot,' she whispered, blowing gently into his nostrils so that he would recognize her by her smell. 'We're going for a ride together, and you'll have to gallop fast, very fast. Would you like that?'

Lancelot butted her chest with his head and began nibbling her dress.

'Does that mean yes?' Igraine whispered as she gently pushed the horse's big nose aside. Then she slipped out of the box again and set off in search of Bertram, but the Master of Horse was nowhere to be found.

'Jost!' she called quietly when one of the grooms passed her. She had often seen him riding Lancelot. 'Hi, Jost, where's Bertram?'

Alarmed, the groom grabbed her arm and hurried her into the harness room.

'Are you mad, coming here?' he asked angrily, as they huddled in the darkest corner among saddles and bridles. 'The new master's had criers going everywhere to proclaim that your family are all witches and black magicians, and you've changed his men into fish for no good reason. Do you want him to throw you into the Dungeon of Despair?'

'No, definitely not.' Igraine took a halter from its hook and put it in the egg basket. 'I'm looking for Bertram. Where is he?'

'Bertram?' Jost looked very gloomy indeed. 'He's in the dungeon already.'

'Wh-what?' stammered Igraine. 'Why?'

'Osmund's castellan saw him go out riding the day before yesterday,' whispered Jost. 'He sent a man after him, and when Bertram came back from Pimpernel he was arrested for treachery.'

'Oh, no!' groaned Igraine.

'You'd better get back to Pimpernel fast!' hissed Jost. 'Darkrock is no place for you these days!'

And then he was gone, and Igraine stood in the dark harness room wondering what to do.

Could a girl who truly wanted to be a knight leave a

friend languishing in the Dungeon of Despair – a friend who was there only because he'd warned her family against an enemy? No!

She fetched her donkey, who was having a fight with one of the ponies, and set off for the prison tower.

Fortunately she knew her way around Darkrock very well, but too many of the maids and grooms knew her, so she kept her head bent as she made her way to the inner courtyard. She was in luck, and no one called her name or grabbed her arm, but as she entered the courtyard the Spiky Knight came towards her, with five other knights following him.

Go on! she ordered her legs, but they refused to obey, and the Spiky Knight passed so close to her that his sword almost brushed her dress.

'Right, this shouldn't take too long,' he said to the other knights. 'Pass the word on. As soon as the catapults arrive we attack that ridiculous castle. Get your fat donkey out of my way, girl.'

Head still bent, Igraine pulled the donkey aside. Her heart was thudding so hard that she thought the Spiky Knight was bound to hear it. But he didn't even look at her.

'With those Singing Books,' she heard him say, 'Osmund will be more powerful than the King himself, and the whole land will belong to us, all the way to the Giant's Hills.'

Go on, Igraine, she told herself again, go on! And this time her legs obeyed, although her knees were still trembling when the prison tower cast its shadow at her feet. Never in her twelve years of life had anyone scared Igraine as much as the Spiky Knight.

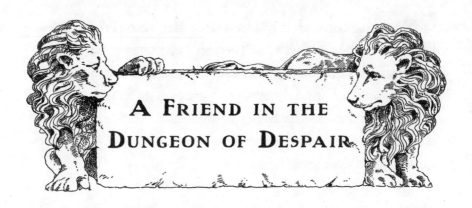

A Friend in the
Dungeon of Despair

he prison tower lay at the end of a dark yard right
behind the castle armouries. Only a single guard
stood in front of it, a tall, thin man who was
picking his teeth with a small stick and looked bored.

'Only one,' Igraine murmured to herself, observing him
from a distance. 'That shouldn't be too difficult.' Before
she left, Albert had taught her ten magic spells for all
kinds of different situations. One of them was sure to do
the trick.

'I'll need your help, Greycoat,' she whispered in the
donkey's ear. 'And no braying,' she added, for Greycoat
enjoyed a good long, loud 'Hee-haw!' 'Or they'll make you
into donkey sausage and I'll end up stuck in the Dungeon
of Despair with Bertram, understand?'

The donkey snorted scornfully, but when Igraine
walked up to the guard he followed her like a lamb.

'Good day,' said Igraine, bobbing a curtsey. 'I'm
supposed to be delivering my eggs here.'

'Nonsense!' growled the man, spitting. 'Does this look like the kitchen?'

Igraine scrutinized the tower, frowning. 'How would I know?'

The guard twisted his mouth in a mocking smile. 'This is the dungeon, little one. The prisoners here don't get anything as nice as fresh eggs to eat.'

'The dungeon?' whispered Igraine, going to a great deal of trouble to sound immensely impressed. 'Ooh, is there anyone in there?'

'You bet. Or why do you think I'm cooling my heels standing around here?' growled the guard. 'Now clear out!'

But Igraine put the basket of eggs down and gave him a beaming smile. 'The Sleeping Beauty,' she whispered. 'Yes, that ought to do it. How does it go, now?'

'What's all that you're whispering?' growled the guard, levelling his spear at her. 'I said clear out!'

However, Igraine didn't move an inch. Following Albert's instructions, she stared straight at the guard's forehead and began murmuring:

'Slumber now like Sleeping Beauty,
Forget your post, forget your duty.
Your eyelids droop, you fall asleep,
May your rest be sound and deep.
Wondrous dreams your mind shall cloud
Until you hear me laugh aloud.'

After the first line the guard's eyes were already closing, and when Igraine had finished reciting the spell he was snoring.

'Keep quiet, do!' Igraine whispered, and she pinched his nose until his snores stopped. Then she closed his visor so that no one would see he was asleep, wedged his spear under his arm to keep him from falling over – and opened the tower door. It was only bolted. Igraine hauled the donkey in and kicked the door shut behind them.

It was dark inside the tower. Daylight filtered in only through a couple of narrow stone slits. Igraine had been here once before, a few months ago, when the Baroness had asked her to count the barrels of honey beer. Igraine had been happy to help, though it had been tough to let herself down into the deep hole, guessing how many spiders were lurking in the dark. She still shuddered at the memory – and prayed that the spiders had left the Dungeon of Despair along with the barrels.

'Come on, Greycoat,' she whispered, hauling the reluctant donkey towards the edge of the hole. A large basket hung over it, fastened to a winch. Igraine took away the two planks that were acting as a makeshift cover for the hole and leaned cautiously over the abyss. The donkey rolled his eyes in alarm and tugged at his halter.

'Bertram?' whispered Igraine into the pitch-black darkness. A sweetish smell rose to her nostrils. The dungeon still had a strong aroma of honey beer.

All was quiet for a few moments. Then Bertram's incredulous voice came up from the depths. 'Igraine? Oh, Lord, I'm hearing ghosts now. It must be the lack of food.'

Igraine laughed quietly. 'No, Bertram, word of knightly honour!' she whispered into the abyss. 'I'm not a ghost. I'm going to lower the basket. Mind it doesn't hit you on the head!'

The winch creaked as Igraine turned the handle, but the basket went slowly down on its rope and disappeared into the darkness.

'Good heavens, it really is you, Igraine!' cried Bertram from below. 'But how are you going to pull me up? I'll be much too heavy for you.'

'I have my donkey here!' replied Igraine. 'I'm going to tie the rope to him so that he can haul you up. Quick, get into the basket.' She went as close to the hole's edge as she could, put out her arm to untie the rope from the winch – and snatched her hand back in alarm.

A fat spider was busy spinning its silvery web around the winch. It had hairy legs and a pale pattern on its back, and this time it wasn't one of the magic spiders that Albert conjured up! Igraine bit her lip, put her hand out once more for the rope – and withdrew it again hastily when the spider came scuttling down its web. It moved so quickly on all those legs!

'Igraine!' called Bertram. 'Can't the donkey do it? Oh, dear, I knew I was too fat.'

'There . . . there's a spider under the winch,' said Igraine in a thread of a voice. 'A huge, hairy spider.'

'A spider? My goodness, Igraine!' You could hear Bertram's sigh rise from the bottom of the pit. 'Blow it away.'

'Blow it away?' murmured Igraine, nervously pulling her hair back from her forehead.

She narrowed her eyes, took a deep breath and – it worked! When she opened her eyes again, the cobweb was torn and the spider had gone.

With shaking fingers, she unfastened the rope from the winch and tied it round the donkey. Then, clicking her tongue, she led Greycoat away from the hole. The little donkey had to pull hard. Bertram was no lightweight, and twice the donkey just stopped and left him dangling over the abyss in the rocking basket. But by pushing and shoving, scolding and petting, Igraine managed to get him going again.

'Just a tiny bit more!' she whispered to Greycoat. 'Come on, you can do it!' But at that moment they suddenly heard voices outside.

'Don't move!' Igraine hurried over to the door.

'What is it, little donkey?' she heard Bertram calling up. 'Fat Bertram here isn't keen to go back down that horrible hole again!'

'Sssh!' hissed Igraine, putting her ear to the door.

'Hey, take a look at Baldur there, will you?' she heard a hoarse voice from outside say. 'Asleep on duty again. If the Spiky Knight sees him the Dungeon of Despair will have two lodgers soon.'

'So it will.' Another voice laughed mockingly. 'How about we let old Iron Spikes know that the guard he posted outside the dungeon shakes all Darkrock Castle with his snoring? What a joke that would be!'

'Wouldn't it just!' replied the other man. 'Sleep tight, Baldur. You'll soon have a visitor.'

'Oh, drat it!' whispered Igraine as the footsteps went away. In haste she ran back to Greycoat and hauled away until at last the basket emerged from the depths.

'Quick!' she gasped, getting both Bertram and the

basket back on firm ground. 'We have to get out of here! Fast!'

The Master of Horse could hardly keep on his feet. She had to help him out of the basket, and he blinked at her with his eyes half closed. After almost two days in total darkness, even what little light there was in the tower hurt them.

'What are you doing here?' whispered Bertram, leaning on her shoulder. 'Didn't I tell you I'd throw you into the moat with my own hands if you turned up at Darkrock?'

'Oh, yes? Would you rather I let you down into the pit again?' Igraine untied her donkey from the rope and helped Bertram to the door. 'I'm not here for fun. Osmund really did come to see us at Pimpernel Castle, and I need a fast horse. I came to borrow Lancelot.'

'What?' Bertram stared at her blankly.

'I'll explain later. Can you walk?'

Bertram nodded.

'Good.' Igraine took Greycoat's reins and cautiously opened the tower door.

The guard was still snoring, but there was no sign of the Spiky Knight. The castle was more crowded than ever. Men were carrying sacks of flour to the kitchens and driving livestock across the courtyard. Armourers made their way through the milling throng. Igraine led the donkey out into the open and signalled to Bertram to follow her. The Master of Horse glanced at the sleeping guard in disbelief as he squeezed past. Igraine took Greycoat over to a dark corner between the castle wall and the great linden tree. The old Baroness of Darkrock used to hold her court of law under its spreading branches.

'Here,' Igraine whispered to Bertram, taking her cloak out of the bundle which also contained her armour. 'We can't disguise you as a woman, I'm afraid, because of your beard, but perhaps this will do. Take the basket; you can have the donkey as well. Then the guards will think you're a farmer bringing eggs to the castle. They only check up on people coming in at the gate. Outside there are so many donkeys and carts that you won't attract attention. You just mustn't seem to be in too much of a hurry.'

Bertram nodded, and put the cloak round his shoulders. It was far too small for him, but better than nothing.

'He's not here yet!' Igraine anxiously looked around. 'But I'd better wake the guard all the same, to be on the safe side. If the Spiky Knight realizes you've gone we'll never get out of the castle. So,' she looked encouragingly at him, 'make me laugh.'

'Make you what?' Bertram cast her an incredulous look. But Igraine didn't answer. The Spiky Knight had appeared under the arched gateway leading to the castle forecourt. There were two soldiers with him, presumably the men whose voices she had heard outside the tower door. They pointed to the tower, but with so many people about the guard was out of sight.

'Bertram, quick!' Igraine urged him. 'Make me laugh! Or the Spiky Knight will throw us both into that awful dungeon.'

The Master of Horse turned pale. The soldiers were clearing a path through the crowd for the Spiky Knight.

'Bertram, please!'

He did his best: he squinted down his nose, waggled his ears, puffed out his cheeks. But none of it raised more than a forced smile from Igraine, and she cursed Albert for casting a spell that couldn't be broken any other way.

The Spiky Knight pushed past two merchants arguing with each other. Only a few more metres, and he would be in front of the guard and notice that he was deep in a very peculiar kind of sleep.

'Sorry,' said Bertram, 'but there's no alternative.' And before Igraine realized what he was doing, he had grabbed her and started tickling her tummy. Her laughter rang out all over the courtyard, and the Spiky Knight glanced round, startled. But at the same moment the guard outside the tower opened his visor and looked around him, bewildered. He was horrified to see the Spiky Knight in front of him, but the castellan had already turned to the two men who had brought him, with a dark expression on his face, and Igraine quickly pulled Bertram away.

'Ride to Pimpernel!' she whispered as they made their way back to the forecourt. 'You'll be safe there. And tell

Albert that Osmund's going to attack as soon as he gets his catapults.'

Bertram sighed, but he nodded. 'And what are you planning to do? Why do you need Lancelot?'

'I have to find some giant's hairs,' replied Igraine, pushing past a couple of travelling entertainers who were doing a dance in front of the smiths' forge. 'My parents had a little accident. So now they're pigs with curly tails.'

Bertram sighed again. 'None of this makes any sense to me,' he said. 'But I can tell you how to get safely through the gate with Lancelot. If the guards stop you, just say you have to take him to the waterhole outside the castle. That's the only place where Lancelot will drink, and word of it has probably got around even among the new guards.'

Igraine nodded and stopped in front of the stables.

'Good luck, Greycoat,' she whispered in the donkey's ear. 'Carry Bertram to Pimpernel. I'm afraid he's a bit fatter than me, but when I come home I'll reward you with a whole handful of sugar lumps. Even if they're not good for those yellow teeth of yours.'

By way of answer the donkey nudged her stomach with his hairy head. Igraine took the bundle of armour off his back and removed the bridle from the egg basket. 'Better throw the eggs away,' she whispered to Bertram, handing him the basket. 'It'll look suspicious if you still have your eggs with you when you leave the castle.'

'Clever girl,' the Master of Horse whispered back,

hugging her so hard that he left her breathless. 'I'll tell your parents all about it. I'll let them know what a brave daughter they have, and perhaps even Albert will be so impressed that he won't tease you so often.'

Then he waved to her once again, and strolled towards the castle gate with his head bent, apparently in no hurry. Igraine didn't turn away until he was past the guards. Now it was time to fetch Lancelot.

ESCAPE FROM DARKROCK

Luckily Igraine didn't meet Jost again. She wasn't
sure whether he might give her away out of fear.
Lancelot snorted excitedly as she put the bridle
over his head, but she placed a soothing hand on his nose
and led him out of the stable, looking as if she had done it
countless times before.

No one stopped her. No one shouted, 'Halt! Who goes
there?' as she swung herself up on Lancelot's back once
they were in the yard. She rode unhindered past knights
and cattle dealers, farmers and blacksmiths, and made her
way through the crowd of people thronging in through the
gate in the thick castle walls. At last she just had to pass
the guards posted on the bridge.

But as she was riding the great stallion past them, one
of them roughly seized her reins.

'Stop!' cried the man. 'What have we here? And where
do you think you're taking that fine horse, girl?'

Igraine clutched the bundle containing her armour and

looked at him as fearlessly as possible. 'To the waterhole, where do you think? He won't drink anywhere else.'

'Is that so?' The guard patted the stallion's neck admiringly, and turned to the other men. 'Ever seen this horse before? Rather too handsome to be in the care of a little girl, wouldn't you say?'

'It's that old devil Lancelot,' one of the guards called back. 'Jost looks after him. Better send for Jost.'

Jost . . . Igraine tore the reins out of the guard's hand and dug her heels into Lancelot's sides. The stallion put back his ears, reared so violently that she almost slid off his back, and galloped away. Some farmers with carts full of fruit were coming over the drawbridge towards them. The horses pulling the carts shied as Lancelot raced on. A farmer jumped into the moat as one of the carts tipped over. Mountains of fruit rolled over the bridge, but with one great leap Lancelot jumped over them and was galloping on. Igraine ducked low over his outstretched neck. His hooves thundering, the stallion stormed off the bridge and past the watchtowers that rose to the sky on both sides of it. The guards on the towers were aiming their catapults ready to fire, but Lancelot charged on through the dealers and farmers bringing their livestock down the road to the castle, through the crowd of jugglers and beggars and soldiers. They all scattered, screaming, and made way for the snorting stallion.

'Turn west, Lancelot!' cried Igraine, swinging him

round. 'We have to go west!' But when she looked back she saw two horsemen in pursuit of them. One was clearing himself a path through the screaming crowd with his sword, the other was drawing his crossbow. Drat it! she thought. Today of all days I have to be wearing skirts!

But just as the first arrow flew past Igraine's shoulder Lancelot swerved off the road and galloped over the bleak, treeless plain surrounding the castle. None of their pursuers' horses could match his speed, and Lancelot carried Igraine off, far, far away from the towers of Darkrock and towards the dark hills where the giant lived.

THE
GIANT GARLEFF

I graine rode until night fell and stars came out in the
sky above the hilltops. Only once did she stop for
a short rest, to let Lancelot drink and graze and to
get into her armour. They met no one on their way, and
the only sounds they heard were the voices of animals in
the dark. Two little dragons barely half Lancelot's size
crossed Igraine's path, and once she saw a herd of unicorns
drinking at a river. When the moon rose, and the world
was all blue and black, Igraine finally reached the hills
where the giant Garleff lived.

'Just look for his footprints,' her father had said. 'You
can't miss them.' And to make doubly sure, Albert had
given her a small bag of silver dust. If Igraine let just a
little of it fall to the ground as she rode, all the tracks
there began to shine – every print left by a paw, a hoof or
a foot – and the fresher the tracks were, the brighter they
shone.

Before long Igraine came upon some gigantic footprints.

It had been raining in the hills, and water collected in the deep hollows left by Garleff's toes and the soles of his feet. Whenever Igraine saw some of these curiously shaped puddles, she sprinkled a pinch of Albert's silver dust into it. And the further she rode, the brighter the trails shone. The bushes covering the slopes were prickly, but giants have thick skins, and Igraine's parents had told her that Garleff liked to stretch out among the thorns by night to look at the stars. When he did that you couldn't see him at all. His huge body disappeared into the thickets of thorns as if the earth had swallowed him up.

In a particularly dark valley, where the starry sky was like a tent spread over the earth, Igraine found giant's tracks that shone brighter than all the rest. She reined Lancelot in and looked around her. No sound met her ears but the song of the night birds and the rushing of water far away.

'Garleff?' she called into the darkness.

Lancelot lowered his head to the grass, which was wet with dew. His nostrils flared as he sniffed the air for scents.

'It's me, Garleff!' called Igraine. 'The daughter of Sir Lamorak and the Fair Melisande. It's Igraine! My father's magic cured you of a nasty rash long ago, do you remember? Now we need your help!'

Nothing stirred. The hills lay silent in the darkness of the night.

Igraine patted Lancelot's neck. 'He doesn't seem to be

here,' she said softly. 'Come on, let's try the next valley.'

But just as she took up the horse's reins again, there was a rustling on the hill to her left, and out of the undergrowth rose a figure so large that its moonlit shadow fell over the whole valley.

Lancelot whinnied and stepped back, his legs trembling.

'Take it easy!' Igraine told him. 'Take it easy, there's nothing to fear.' But she herself felt her stomach twist with alarm. She had heard hundreds and hundreds of stories about giants, but she'd never before seen one in front of her in flesh and blood. When she dared to look up, she saw Garleff's right shoulder cover the moon.

'Oho, oho! So it's the daughter of Lamorak the Wily!' he said. His voice was deep and full, like a warm wind blowing down on Igraine. The giant took one leg out of the thorny undergrowth, and with a mighty tread he climbed down the slope of the hill, until he was so close to her that when she glanced up at him she was looking straight into his nostrils.

'Help?' boomed Garleff. 'What do you need my help for, little human?'

Igraine put a hand on Lancelot's trembling flank.

'I need some of your hairs!' she called up to the giant. 'Four or five would be enough, that's what my parents said.'

'Giant's hairs?' Garleff crouched down. He gently picked Igraine off Lancelot's back, and put her on his knee. 'Have those two gone and bewitched themselves?'

Igraine looked into Garleff's brown giant's eyes and nodded. 'They've turned themselves into pigs,' she said. 'It doesn't bother me and my brother too much, so long as it's not for ever, but now they're pigs they can't cast spells, and just at this moment someone's come along trying to steal our Books of Magic. Are you with me so far?'

'Hm,' said the giant, nodding his head back and forth. 'I'm not entirely sure, but go on.'

'His name is Osmund, and he's our new neighbour,' Igraine went on. 'He and his castellan are mustering a huge army to attack Pimpernel. That's why I'm in such a terrible hurry. I have to bring my parents some giant's hairs so that they can turn themselves back into their real shape and cast a spell to change Osmund into a cockroach or a woodlouse. Which would serve him right, believe you me!'

The giant looked up at the sky. He went on gazing at it for quite a time, so long that Igraine was beginning to think he'd forgotten all about her. But finally the giant looked back at her.

'I don't often help human beings,' he said, scratching his ear. Igraine could have taken a seat in it quite comfortably. 'I don't really understand them, if you see what I mean. All that chasing about, all that fuss and bother – and your squeaky little voices. They make me all nervous and edgy. Luckily humans don't often venture here. But your father did cure me of my rash. It itched horribly – it even spoiled my pleasure in the stars – and giants never forget a good deed, or a bad one either. So you shall have my hairs.' Gently, he picked Igraine up between his thumb and forefinger and put her on his head. 'Help yourself, Igraine, Lamorak's daughter.'

Each of Garleff's hairs was as thick as the quill of a goose's feather, and Igraine sank up to her chin in them. Taking out her sword, she cut off a bunch as long as her arm, rolled them up and carefully put it in the bag she wore at her belt.

'Ready!' she called, and the giant picked her out of his hair and put her on the palm of his hand.

He looked thoughtfully at her, as if she were a butterfly who had fluttered down to settle on him. 'That story you told me,' he growled, rubbing his mighty nose, 'I don't like the sound of it. And I don't like to think of you riding through these hills all on your own. You're rather small, you know, not much larger than my big toe. And there are some really bad people between the hills and the Whispering Woods. I can't come with you myself. I never leave these hills. It's only too easy for us giants to tread on the people we want to help and squash them flat. But I know someone who could go with you and perhaps even help you against this man – what was his name again?'

'Osmund,' replied Igraine.

'Exactly.' Garleff nodded thoughtfully and lapsed into silence.

'Yes,' he murmured much later. 'I think it wouldn't be a bad idea to ask him.'

'Ask who?' enquired Igraine.

'You'll soon see,' replied Garleff. He took Igraine in one hand, and Lancelot (who didn't like it at all) in the other, and stood up. Then he marched away with mighty strides over the hills into the dark night, going east.

THE SORROWFUL
KNIGHT

arleff carried Igraine to the foot of a mountain
that rose bleak and rocky into the starry sky. Even
Garleff looked small beside it. A long, long flight
of steps carved in the rock led up to a tower that clung to
the grey side of the mountain like a swallow's nest.

Garleff carefully deposited Igraine and Lancelot on the
wet grass, bent down, and put his finger to his lips. 'Hear
that?' he asked softly.

Igraine listened, and heard a sigh, a deep sigh carried
down to her from the tower by the wind.

'It's like that day and night,' the giant whispered. 'Sad
and sorrowful, he's always sad and sorrowful. Yet he
was once a great knight. He saw off two giant-hunters
for me, and he's often saved the unicorns from hunting
parties. He won countless fights. He unhorsed dozens of
knights at the king's tournaments, and he won the whole
tournament six times and was rewarded with a kiss from
the princess. But one day he returned to these hills with

the most sorrowful countenance in the world. He didn't
go back to his own castle, which is only one valley away,
and he asked me to let him build this poor tower instead.
He cut the steps out of the rock himself, working until his
hands were bleeding. And ever since then he's been sighing
night and day. He says he's lost his honour and he can
never show his face among men and women again. But I'm
sure he'd keep you company on the way home if you asked
for his help. If his eternal sighing doesn't drive you mad,
that is.'

Igraine looked up at the lonely tower.

'I always wanted to meet a knight who'd won one of the
royal tournaments,' she said softly. 'Do you really think
he'd come with me?'

'I'm sure he would!' Garleff lowered his voice a little
more. 'To be honest, I think it would do him good to help
someone again. Wait here. I'll go and ask him.'

The giant stood up, took a long stride towards the
mountain, and peered through the top window of the
tower.

'Hello?' he called. 'Hello, anyone at home?'

Nothing moved on the other side of the window, but a
figure rose behind the moonlit battlements on the tower
roof. It was the knight. His armour shone, but not so
much as a single plume adorned his helmet.

'Oh, is that you, Garleff?' Igraine heard him say sadly.
'What do you want, my friend?'

'I have a girl with me who rode to these hills all alone from the Whispering Woods to get some of my hairs. She arrived safely, but it would set my mind at rest if you could escort her home.' The giant thrust his enormous nose over the battlements. 'Her name is Igraine, and her parents' castle is being threatened by a nasty piece of work called Osmund.'

'Osmund?' said the knight. 'Oh, I know that name. And I've heard no good of him either. He's an enchanter, one of the black magicians.' He leaned over the battlements and looked down at Igraine. 'She's wearing a suit of armour,' he said in surprise.

'She's a brave little thing,' said Garleff, 'but all the same, I'd like to think she had an experienced knight's company on her way home, if you see what I mean.'

The knight said nothing. He went on saying nothing for a small eternity. Then he sighed again. 'In truth,' he said, 'a knight must help a damsel in distress, even a knight who has lost his honour.'

'Oh, for the stars' sake, don't go on about that again!' said Garleff, lifting the sighing knight off the top of his tower.

Lancelot snorted when the giant put the knight down on the grass next to him, but he bravely stood his ground behind Igraine.

'Noble lady,' said the knight, bowing to her, 'I am the Sorrowful Knight of the Mount of Tears, and as you are obviously in dire straits I offer you my services.'

'Th-th-that's very nice of you!' stammered Igraine. 'Really. Er – could you come right away? You see, I'm in rather a hurry.'

'As you wish,' replied the knight. 'Let me just call my noble steed.'

He gave a low whistle, and a grey mare appeared between the trees. The sight of the giant didn't seem to alarm her. She trotted up to the Sorrowful Knight at her leisure and stopped in front of him. The mare was saddled and bridled as if for a tournament.

'Come now, Grey,' said the knight. 'The noble Igraine needs our protection, so we will go adventuring once more.' The horse whinnied softly as the knight swung himself up on her back. Lancelot pricked up his ears, curious. Igraine made sure once again that the giant's hairs were safe in the bag at her belt, then she picked up Lancelot's reins.

'Thank you, Garleff!' she called up to the giant. 'Thank you for everything!'

Garleff knelt down on the grass in front of her and carefully shook her hand, which was smaller than his fingernail. 'My regards to your parents!' he said. 'And tell them to be a little more careful casting their spells from now on.'

'I'll do that,' said Igraine.

Then she mounted Lancelot, waved back one last time, and rode away beside the Sorrowful Knight.

Garleff watched them go for some time, and did not lie down on the thorny hillside again to look at the stars until they were out of sight.

THE RULES OF CHIVALRY

The knight's grey mare was not quite as fast as Lancelot, but they made good progress. Nothing stopped them in their swift ride. The night was quiet and peaceful, and the sky was full of stars.

The Sorrowful Knight was a silent companion. Igraine asked him about the tournaments he had won, the hunters he had driven away, the unicorns he had saved. She asked why he didn't have a squire, and what the king's daughter looked like close up. But the knight just sighed, murmured sometimes, 'Yes,' sometimes, 'No,' and now and then simply, 'I forget.' Igraine, however, had dreamed for so long of riding beside a real knight one day that she went on asking questions. What did the coat of arms on his shield mean, she asked. Did he prefer fighting with a sword or a battleaxe; was the king really as useless at tilting with a lance as people said? That question made the knight laugh. And finally he began talking.

By the time they left the Giant's Hills behind, and

reached the marshy plain that stretched all the way to the Whispering Wood, the sun had risen and Igraine had learned quite a lot about the knight's adventures. But she hadn't yet found out why he was so sad.

'How much further is it to your parents' castle?' asked the Sorrowful Knight as they watered their horses at the Elfin River that was said to flow all the way to the sea.

'Oh, it can't be much further now,' Igraine said, yawning. 'If we don't stop to rest we can be there just after sunset.' Her stomach was rumbling, and she was dreadfully tired after the long, endless ride, but she couldn't wait to be home again.

'We should rest our horses,' said the knight, and slipped out of the saddle. 'Nothing hostile has met us yet, but it still may, and in that case our horses had better not have weary legs.'

Igraine could hardly disagree with that, and Lancelot was obviously pleased when she let him wade in the clear water of the river. But Igraine herself could think of nothing but Pimpernel Castle. Had Osmund attacked already? Suppose she came too late?

'I am rather worried, you know,' she told the Sorrowful Knight softly.

'And I fear you have good reason,' he said. 'Tell me more about this man Osmund.'

'He's our new neighbour. His castle is east of Pimpernel. In fact all our neighbours are horrible now, because to the west there's the One-Eyed Duke, and he has a bad reputation too.'

'Yes, I have never heard anyone speak well of him.' The Sorrowful Knight drew his sword and ran his finger over the blade. 'Well, what do you say? I see you carry a sword. Would you care for a little passage at arms to loosen up our weary limbs?'

'Really?' Igraine leaped to her feet.

Swordplay with a real knight! So far she had never fought anyone but the leather dummy, the grooms at Darkrock or Bertram, and Bertram wasn't exactly quick on his feet. She drew the sword she had brought. It was short and not too heavy, as if made for Igraine's hand. The words engraved on the blade said that it had been a present to her great-grandfather on his thirteenth birthday.

'If you will allow me,' said the knight, 'I'll choose a long dagger as my weapon. My sword is clumsy and awkward compared to yours.'

'Of course, whatever you like,' replied Igraine, getting into position. 'Shall I put my helmet on?'

The knight smiled. 'That won't be necessary. You're fighting a friend,' he said.

Igraine's heart was in her mouth as she countered his first attack. After she had parried his blade for the third time, the Sorrowful Knight stopped in surprise. 'Well done!' he said. 'My word, you're not at all bad!'

Igraine felt the blood shoot into her face. 'Well, I've had quite a lot of practice,' she faltered.

'Good. Then now I'll show you a few things that you may not have practised yet,' said the Sorrowful Knight – and he didn't seem quite so sorrowful any more.

They fenced and fenced while the horses grazed by the riverbank and rested their tired legs. At last Igraine mopped the sweat off the end of her nose, gasped for air, and let herself drop into the grass. 'I can't go on,' she said.

The knight sat down on a stone beside her and smiled. 'You fight very skilfully for your age,' he said. 'Even experienced squires are slower. But always remember the two rules of chivalry: never turn your skill with the sword against weaker opponents, use it only in self-defence – and never use it to enrich yourself.'

'Of course not,' said Igraine, sitting up again.

'Good,' said the Sorrowful Knight, and he looked at her thoughtfully. 'Then let me tell you two more rules that you may not have heard before. Always remember that your opponent may not be keeping to the rules himself, and remember,' he added, bending his head, 'that you will never be as good as the knight who does nothing day in, day out, but practise fighting.'

Igraine looked at him, taken aback. 'But I want to be the very, very best knight of all,' she said in a low voice.

'And spend the rest of your life practising fighting? Every hour of every day?'

Igraine stroked her gleaming armour. 'Well, perhaps not every hour,' she said.

'But that is what some knights do,' said the Sorrowful Knight. 'I myself once knew such a knight . . .' And he drove his sword into the ground.

'I bet that Iron Hedgehog practises all day, every day!' said Igraine. 'He has iron spikes all over his armour, and his face is as white as snow. As if he never takes his helmet off.'

The Sorrowful Knight looked at her in astonishment. 'What are you saying? What knight do you mean?'

'He's Osmund's castellan.' Igraine knelt down by the bank of the river, cupped her hands and filled them with cool water. 'It gives you goosebumps just to look at him. Well, not me. I'm not afraid of him, I mean . . .' She cleared her throat, embarrassed. 'I mean, the only thing I'm really

frightened of is spiders. I know it's stupid, but – is there anything you're afraid of?'

The Sorrowful Knight didn't answer. He took his sword out of the ground, wiped it clean, and put it back in the sheath. Then he sighed.

'I am indeed afraid of certain things, noble Igraine,' he said at last. 'But I fear nothing in the world more than the knight of whom you spoke just now. His name is Rowan Heartless. He is the man who robbed me of my honour. I have challenged him to joust three times since then, and each time he defeated me with his first lance-thrust. I will keep my word and escort you back to your parents' castle, but I can't help you against Heartless. No one can.'

'Well, we'll see about that,' said Igraine, straightening up again. 'How did he rob you of your honour? Not just by defeating you?'

'No, a knight does not lose his honour when he is defeated in fair fight. He did worse, much worse, and I became the Sorrowful Knight of the Mount of Tears.'

'Oh, come on!' Igraine reached for his hand. 'It can't be as bad as all that. But you don't have to tell me about it if you don't want to. Just come to Pimpernel with me and you can watch my parents turn Osmund and the Spiky Knight into tadpoles or woodlice. They need the giant's hairs for that, however, because they're pigs at the moment, I'm afraid. Very pretty pigs, though.'

A tiny smile appeared on the Sorrowful Knight's lips.

'I suppose magic isn't allowed in chivalry, is it?' asked Igraine.

'No. That would be dishonourable,' replied the knight.

'Well, never mind.' Igraine went over to Lancelot and put his bridle on again. 'I'm very bad at remembering magic spells anyway. Let's ride on, and you can tell me what else is dishonourable.'

'As you wish, brave Igraine,' said the Sorrowful Knight, mounting his horse. 'Do you know, I am sure you will be an excellent knight some day.'

THE
ONE-EYED DUKE

Igraine dared not ride past Darkrock carrying the precious giant's hairs. So they turned west, where the One-Eyed Duke ruled the land and its people. Neither Igraine nor the Sorrowful Knight had ever ridden this way, but Igraine knew that the Elfin River would lead them to the Whispering Woods.

Soon dense woods came down to the banks of the river. They offered protection from prying eyes, but progress was slower among the trees than in the hills. The horses grew restless; they picked up the acrid scent of bears and wolves. Igraine and the knight had their swords at the ready, but apart from a couple of robbers who made off at the sight of their armour, nothing but hares and deer crossed their path.

It was a hot day, but under the trees it felt cool, and early in the afternoon Igraine saw the duke's castle on a hill not far away. It was surrounded by miserable straw huts, and the peasants with their children were toiling away in the fields outside, sweating in the baking sun.

Igraine reined in her horse. 'Look at that,' she said. 'Even the children have to work from sunrise to sunset while the duke goes out hunting. I wouldn't want to end up that sort of knight.'

The Sorrowful Knight smiled. He was smiling more and more often now.

'I hardly think we need worry about that, noble Igraine,' he said.

They went on following the river. Soon it made its way, foaming, through a ravine with steep and densely overgrown sides. Only a narrow path led along it above the water.

'Why don't you live in your castle any more?' Igraine asked the knight as they followed the path side by side. 'It must be terribly cold and draughty in that tower.' And there were probably any number of spiders, but presumably the knight didn't mind them.

For some time he didn't answer. And when he finally did, his voice was dark with sadness. 'I was once the guardian of a castle,' he said. 'Three ladies lived there, and I was appointed to protect them.'

'What for? Couldn't they protect themselves?' asked Igraine.

'They weren't like you,' replied the knight.

'What became of them?'

There was another long pause. Then the knight said,

'Rowan Heartless, whom you call the Spiky Knight, stole them away, and I could do nothing to stop him.'

'Oh!' Igraine looked at him in dismay. 'But how could they just let themselves be stolen away like that?'

The knight never got around to answering her. There was a rustling in the bushes on the slope to their left. Lancelot shied away as something slithered down the ravine with a loud squawk. It landed in front of the stallion's hooves in a shower of leaves and twigs that had been torn loose, rolled on and fell into the river with a mighty splash.

'What was that?' asked Igraine, bending over Lancelot's neck.

Three heads emerged from the river, spluttering, the third one noticeably smaller than the other two. They all belonged to a moss-green dragon which hauled itself out of the water, snorting angrily, and stared grimly up at Igraine and the Sorrowful Knight.

'Oh, no! Two more of them!' growled the smallest head. 'It's one of those days again.'

'What are you gaping at?' bellowed the other two heads. 'Are you out hunting dragons for fun too? Do you need a dragon's head to hang over your castle gate? Look at my third head, will you? The One-Eyed Duke cut it off, and it still hasn't grown back any larger than one of your silly human heads. I really am sick and tired of this. And today that fellow's after me again! Don't you and your sort in those tinpot helmets have anything better to do? What the . . .'

'We don't hunt dragons!' Igraine interrupted as soon as she could get a word in. 'Really we don't. Word of knightly honour!'

'I wouldn't give much for that!' growled the dragon back. 'But I don't fancy sitting about in this icy water any longer either.'

It sneezed three times as it waded to land, going red in its three green faces, and once on the bank it shook itself so vigorously that Lancelot almost bolted. The Sorrowful Knight's mare, however, seemed to be used to dragons.

'Look at me!' muttered the dragon, dragging its tail out of the river and gloomily examining its reflection. 'Ridiculous. Absolutely ridiculous. My head is no bigger than a plum, and if that duke had his way I'd have three heads that size on my neck!'

Its scaly body was so large that it entirely blocked the path between the slope and the river. Igraine was just wondering how they were ever going to get past it when the Sorrowful Knight turned in his saddle.

'There's someone coming,' he told her softly. 'Draw your sword.'

Igraine obeyed. She heard the sound of galloping hooves, the clank of armour, and dogs barking.

The dragon hunched all three heads down between its shoulders in alarm. 'I know who that is!' it hissed. 'I just

can't seem to shake him off. I suppose I'll have to wave
goodbye to another head now!'

'No, you won't,' said Igraine, turning Lancelot so that
he was standing in front of the dripping wet dragon. The
Sorrowful Knight brought his horse up beside her, and
laid his sword over his knees. Igraine did the same.

'What's all this about?' asked the dragon, taken aback.

'We will protect you, fire-worm,' replied the Sorrowful Knight. 'Or have you ever done the One-Eyed Duke wrong?'

'Of course not,' cried the dragon. 'I've never done a living soul wrong. I haven't cut off one of anyone's heads! I feed on moonlight, and all I want is to lie in my cave and be left in peace.'

'Indeed, that is not too much to ask,' said the Sorrowful Knight.

'Here he comes!' cried Igraine.

Four hounds, barking, raced down the path. Behind them galloped a knight on a large horse, which was also wearing armour. The rider's visor was open, and Igraine saw that he wore an eye patch embroidered with pearls. The coat of arms on his shield was a dragon's head. When the hounds saw the strange knights they stopped in surprise, growled and put their ears back. Their master, taken aback, reined his horse in.

'Out of my way, you!' he roared. 'That's my dragon. I've been after it for weeks. What's more, you're trespassing on my property. So clear off, and get a move on!'

The hounds growled louder than ever and cautiously ventured a little closer.

'Run for it, dragon,' said Igraine over her shoulder, without taking her eyes off the duke. 'And if you want to be rid of this one-eyed idiot for ever, move to the Whispering Woods. No one hunts dragons there.'

The dragon's three pairs of eyes looked incredulously down at her. Then it turned and scuttled away as fast as its scaly legs would carry it.

'Stop! Stop, blast you!' bellowed the One-Eyed Duke, so angry that he almost fell off his horse. 'You two will be sorry for this! That was the only three-headed dragon in my forests!'

With a brusque movement he drew his sword, waved it over his head, uttered a loud roar and stormed forward.

'Leave this to me,' the Sorrowful Knight whispered to Igraine. Without waiting for her answer, he raised his shield and urged his horse on along the narrow path to meet the One-Eyed Duke.

The duke slammed his sword down on the Sorrowful Knight's shield so furiously that Igraine could hardly see or hear for the noise. But the Sorrowful Knight didn't seem particularly impressed. Effortlessly, he fended off the wild sword-strokes, then suddenly lowered his shield. The duke immediately went at the target so easily offered, and the Sorrowful Knight answered with a blow that struck the sword from his hand. It flew through the air and landed in the river. The duke, taken aback, watched it go – and fell backwards off his horse when the Sorrowful Knight dealt him another blow on the breastplate. His hounds licked his face as he landed among them, and his horse jumped into the river, swam to the opposite bank and stood there with its reins dangling.

The Sorrowful Knight rode over to his fallen opponent, dismounted and looked down at him. 'Do you require my help?' he asked.

'No!' shouted the One-Eyed Duke. 'You were lucky, that's all! Tell me your name, so that I can find you and take revenge for this disgrace!'

Without a word, Igraine's companion put his sword back in its scabbard and remounted his horse. 'I am the Sorrowful Knight of the Mount of Tears,' he said. 'And you, less than noble knight, surely do not know the meaning of disgrace.'

So saying he turned his grey mare, rode back to Igraine, and with a weary wave of his hand gestured to her to follow him.

'You just leave the dragons alone in future, understand?' called Igraine to the duke, who was still lying among his hounds. 'If I ever hear otherwise, you'll have me to deal with. Or I'll tell my mother to turn you into a fat worm.'

The duke could think of no answer to that, and Igraine turned Lancelot and rode after the Sorrowful Knight.

THE CASTLE
UNDER SIEGE

I t was pitch dark by the time they reached Pimpernel, but even from some way off they could see countless fires burning in the darkness, and when they came closer Igraine realized that hundreds of tents had been pitched on the meadows outside the castle. Osmund's banner was fluttering over the largest tent. Pimpernel was under siege.

The castle walls shone red in the firelight, and glowing sparks were falling to the castle moat from the gargoyles' mouths.

'I fear this does not look good, noble Igraine!' whispered the Sorrowful Knight. 'Your castle, forgive me for saying so, is rather small and rather decrepit. It will not hold out for long against such a large body of troops.'

He looked quite surprised when Igraine laughed. 'Oh, this is nothing,' she whispered back. 'When Accolon Blackbeard besieged Pimpernel there were tents pitched all the way to the horizon. I hadn't been born yet, but my father's told me about it. Our old castle can defend itself quite well. As you see, the bridge is drawn up, the walls and the tower are still standing, and now that I have the giant's hairs, I'm not a bit worried. Once my parents are rid of their curly tails Osmund won't be able to run for it fast enough, I promise you! The only problem they probably have at the moment is provisions, because my brother Albert can turn a stone into a live mouse all right, but when it comes to anything edible he can only summon dry biscuits and blue eggs.'

'Ah.' The Sorrowful Knight glanced at the leaning tower and the rather low castle walls, and didn't seem entirely convinced. 'Well, even if it is as you say,' he added after a while, 'how will you get inside the castle unobserved? Shall I start a fight to distract the attackers' attention?'

'And get yourself taken prisoner?' Igraine energetically shook her head. 'No, certainly not. Getting into Pimpernel is easy. There's an old escape route. My great-grandmother had it built because my great-grandfather Pelleas was always having trouble with other knights, and unfortunately he couldn't work magic at all. Albert and I have often used the tunnel. Its entrance is on the edge of the woods. Come on!'

They had left the horses in a hollow out of sight of the tents, and when Lancelot saw Igraine coming he pawed the ground with his front hoof as if he could hardly wait to set off again. But Igraine regretfully shook her head.

'I'm really grateful for your help,' she whispered to him. 'But I'm afraid you wouldn't fit into the secret passage. Go back to Darkrock – or would you rather not see Osmund again?'

Lancelot took a step backwards and stopped.

'Very well,' said Igraine, taking his reins, 'then I'll take you with me to the outskirts of the wood, and once we're there you can decide. What about you?' she asked, looking at the Sorrowful Knight, who was standing beside her deep in thought, patting his mare. 'Are you sure you won't come into the castle with me?'

The Sorrowful Knight shook his head. 'I would only bring you bad luck.'

'What on earth are you talking about?' Igraine took his hand. 'Just because the Spiky Knight stole those three ladies away? You fought splendidly to protect the three-headed dragon – and come to think of it, where are the ladies now?'

The Sorrowful Knight suppressed a smile. 'I don't know. I never saw them again, though I searched for them everywhere. I challenged Rowan the Heartless three times, to get the answer out of him, but as I have told you, he defeated me every time and kept the secret to himself.'

'Only three times,' said Igraine, mounting Lancelot. 'Three times is nothing. Perhaps it's a case of fourth time lucky. Or even fifth time lucky. You're bound to defeat him some day, and then he'll have to tell you what he did with the ladies. But do please come to our castle with me!'

'No.' The Sorrowful Knight shook his head again. 'No, I will escort you only as far as the entrance to the tunnel, and then we will say goodbye.'

'Oh, well,' murmured Igraine. 'Better than nothing, I suppose.'

And she rode on ahead.

THE MOUTH OF
THE STONE LION

The gargoyles were spitting sparks that lit up the
night like fiery rain. Igraine kept a good distance
from Osmund's camp as she rode round it. She
counted eight men on guard, and was very relieved when
she and the knight finally reached the first trees and the
Whispering Woods swallowed them up.

Osmund hadn't dared to pitch any tents close to the
forest. People told scary stories about it, and obviously
the new lord of Darkrock had heard them. Six mounted
guards were keeping watch on Pimpernel Castle where its
walls faced the Whispering Woods. They had their backs
to the trees, but now and then one of them turned in his
saddle and stared at the forest behind him – as if he feared
that something wild and hungry might leap out of the
dense undergrowth at any moment.

Igraine rode along close to the edge of the woods so that
she could keep an eye on the guards. The leaves of the old
trees rustled above her head, and branches hanging low

brushed her face. The horses didn't like the whispering sound of the forest. They twitched their ears nervously, but Igraine had walked among the trees with Albert so often that she wasn't afraid of the place any more.

'We're nearly there,' she whispered. 'There, look—'

'Wait!' the knight interrupted her sharply, seizing her reins. 'Something is crouching among the trees. A huge animal. Larger than a dragon, I would say. Do you see its hungry eyes?'

But Igraine just laughed. 'That's one of Mama's lions,' she whispered. 'It's made of stone from head to paws. My mother put it there by magic to guard the entrance to the tunnel. Come on.'

Lancelot pranced backwards, but Igraine soothed him, talking quietly until he was prepared to go on again.

The stone lion lay in dappled moonlight. Its head was raised so high towards the leafy treetops that even sitting on horseback Igraine could only just touch its chin. Twining plants grew round its huge body, and its eyes shone like moons caught among the branches.

Igraine slipped out of the saddle, and once again she glanced at the guards by the moat. They still had their backs to her and the knight. But even if they had turned, the shadows under the trees would have hidden them from sight.

With a quick movement, Igraine jumped on to the lion's mossy paw, clambered from there to its mane, and sat down among the stony locks of hair curling around its muzzle.

'Now, watch this,' she whispered, putting out her hand to scratch the lion's nose. A growl came from its chest, and the mighty mouth opened with a slight creaking sound, yawning wider and wider until it could easily have swallowed Igraine up. A flight of steps came into view between the lion's teeth, leading down its throat.

'By Death and a cauldron!' exclaimed the Sorrowful Knight. 'Your mother must be a great enchantress indeed, if she can awake stone to life. It seems I need have no fear for you. So let us say goodbye.' He bent his head. 'Farewell, brave Igraine, and I wish you a safe homecoming to your castle. Meanwhile I will keep watch on those guards.'

So he really wasn't going to come with her. Igraine missed him already, but she did her best not to show it. 'Goodbye, then!' she said. 'But I must just say goodbye to Lancelot.' She scrambled down the lion's back and flung her arms round the horse's neck. 'I'll come and see you again soon,' she whispered, burying her face in the black mane, 'the moment my parents have turned Osmund into something truly repulsive.'

Lancelot nudged her face nervously with his nose and whinnied quietly. Alarmed, Igraine put her hands over his nostrils.

The Sorrowful Knight ducked behind a bush. 'That was unwise!' he whispered. 'A guard is looking this way!'

The guard had swung his horse around and looked hard at the outskirts of the forest. But the night was black as soot among the trees, and after a few endless moments the man turned away again.

'Now, Igraine!' whispered the Sorrowful Knight. 'Go, before his suspicions are aroused again.'

'Yes, yes, I'm off,' she whispered, patting Lancelot's soft muzzle one last time. 'Don't worry, Lancelot, I'll be back to see you, word of knightly honour.'

'Igraine!' said the Sorrowful Knight, without turning round. 'If you do not disappear into that lion's mouth this minute I'll stuff you into it with my own hands!'

'All right, I've gone!' she called back softly. 'But it really is a shame you won't come too.'

By way of answer the Sorrowful Knight only sighed.

For the second time Igraine clambered up the mane as nimbly as a squirrel. It was child's play in her feather-light suit of armour. Lancelot put his ears back anxiously and never took his eyes off her.

'Sssh!' Igraine whispered to him. 'It's all right, this isn't a real mouth.'

But as soon as she put her foot between the stony teeth the great horse flung up his head and neighed with fear: a loud, shrill sound.

The guard closest to them immediately swung his horse round, calling a sharp command to the others. Six

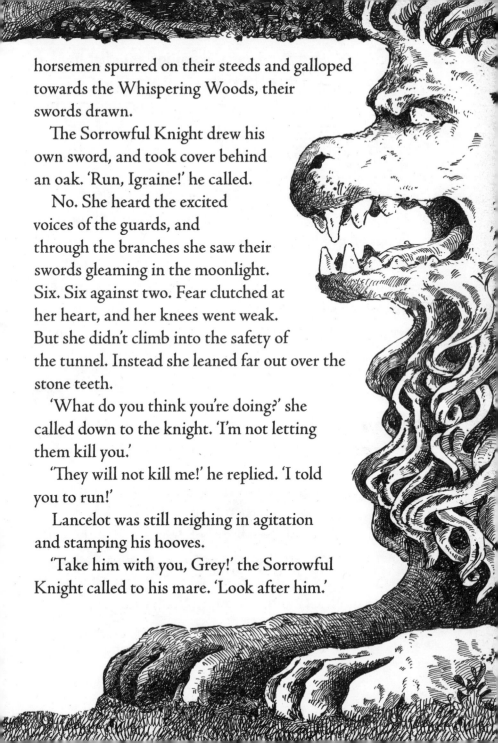

horsemen spurred on their steeds and galloped towards the Whispering Woods, their swords drawn.

The Sorrowful Knight drew his own sword, and took cover behind an oak. 'Run, Igraine!' he called.

No. She heard the excited voices of the guards, and through the branches she saw their swords gleaming in the moonlight. Six. Six against two. Fear clutched at her heart, and her knees went weak. But she didn't climb into the safety of the tunnel. Instead she leaned far out over the stone teeth.

'What do you think you're doing?' she called down to the knight. 'I'm not letting them kill you.'

'They will not kill me!' he replied. 'I told you to run!'

Lancelot was still neighing in agitation and stamping his hooves.

'Take him with you, Grey!' the Sorrowful Knight called to his mare. 'Look after him.'

The mare obeyed. Nudging the stallion with her head, she drove him in among the trees.

'I'm sitting up here until you come too!' Igraine's voice was trembling, but she sounded extremely determined. 'Please! Don't be so pig-headed!'

Osmund's men had almost reached the wood. Igraine could hear the clinking of their chain mail and the snorting of their horses. The Sorrowful Knight closed his visor.

'What on earth do you think you're doing?' cried Igraine in terror. 'They'll carve you out of your armour in slices!'

But by now the guards had already driven their reluctant horses into the wood, making a way through the thorny undergrowth with their swords.

The Sorrowful Knight leaped out of his cover and barred their way.

'Who are you?' shouted one of the men. 'In the name of Osmund the Magnificent, surrender!'

One of the horsemen placed his sword-point threateningly against the Sorrowful Knight's breast. The others were coming up from all sides, but their horses shied once they were under the rustling trees.

'I am the Knight of the Mount of Tears!' called the Sorrowful Knight, striking the guard's sword aside with his shield. 'The Magnificent, do you call your master? I call him Osmund the Greedy, Osmund the Dishonourable.'

Furiously, the guards raised their swords. The Sorrowful Knight parried their blows, but they were sitting safely on their horses, driving him back between the lion's stone paws.

Igraine felt her anger drowning out her fear. 'Don't you touch him!' she shouted, clinging to the stone teeth. With all her might, she struck the helmet off one of the riders with her sword. The blow made him sway in the saddle and put his hands to his head.

'Igraine!' called the Sorrowful Knight. 'I tell you for the last time, run!'

'And I tell you for the last time, I'm not going without you!' Igraine shouted back. 'Come up here this minute, or I shall jump! I'll jump right into the middle of those guards with their tinpot helmets, and if they skewer me it will be all your fault!'

The Sorrowful Knight responded to this with an extremely unchivalrous curse. He drove back his attackers with a couple of sword-strokes, sprang on to one of the lion's paws and then clambered up to the open mouth. With a final leap, he was between the stone teeth, standing beside Igraine. Osmund's men stared up at them in astonishment. They tried to drive their horses between the stone paws, and two of the guards even stood on their saddles to haul themselves up to the lion's mouth, but the horses reared and their riders fell into the thorny undergrowth and got tangled up in brambles.

Finally one soldier tried to climb the mane, but Igraine pushed him off with her foot. Then she jumped right inside the lion's mouth, pulling the Sorrowful Knight in with her, and shouted in as loud a voice as she could muster:

'Stony lion, close your jaws
Rest now on your stony paws.
It was magic made you wake,
Roar once more for magic's sake.'

The deep growl uttered by the stone lion was such a terrifying sound that all the horses threw their riders and galloped away in panic, while the huge lion slowly, very slowly, closed its jaws and wrapped Igraine and the Sorrowful Knight in darkness. They heard Osmund's men clambering up the stone outside and hammering on the lion's nose with their swords. Spear-points pushed between the stone lips, crunching. But the mouth refused to open.

'It is not chivalrous to escape such a battle by flight,' whispered the Sorrowful Knight in the darkness.

'But they'd have slit us open!' said Igraine. 'Six against two – is that what you'd call chivalrous?'

The Sorrowful Knight had to smile. 'Six against one and a half,' he said.

'Oh, all right,' muttered Igraine. 'Anyway, I can't get to be the most famous knight in the world if I let a nasty bunch like that slice me up at the age of twelve, and you're too good for such a fate anyway.'

The Sorrowful Knight sighed once more. Outside,

Osmund's guards were bellowing furiously at each other. 'You are an incredibly pig-headed girl, noble Igraine,' said the knight.

'Yes, that's what Albert always says,' agreed Igraine. 'Come on, I'll lead you down the stairs. I'm afraid it's been dark inside the tunnel since Albert let the glow-worms out because he thought they were unhappy. My brother has a very soft heart when it comes to glow-worms and mice.'

Then she took the Sorrowful Knight's hand and led him down the slippery steps until, by the light of a single glow-worm that had lost its way, they reached the underground tunnel which Igraine's great-grandmother had once had made so that her husband Pelleas could escape from his enemies.

EGG YOLKS AND
APPLE CRUMBS

The courtyard of Pimpernel Castle was dark and deserted when Igraine pushed aside the stone slab that closed the other end of her great-grandfather's escape route. The only lights showing were behind the tower windows. Up on the wall, a solitary figure was leaning over the battlements. It couldn't be Albert; he wasn't nearly so fat.

'Bertram?' Igraine called up to him. 'Bertram, I'm back!'

The Master of Horse spun round and looked incredulously down at the courtyard.

'Igraine!' he called. 'Where on earth have you sprung from? Is all that fuss over in Osmund's camp your doing? The guards are running about like headless chickens!'

Bertram stopped abruptly when the Sorrowful Knight climbed out of the tunnel after Igraine. 'And who's this you've brought with you?' he asked suspiciously.

'The Sorrowful Knight from the Mount of Tears!' replied Igraine. 'He very kindly escorted me home. Where are Albert and my curly-tailed parents? Asleep?'

'No, no one's been getting any sleep around here since Osmund's army set up camp down below.' Bertram hurried down the steps. 'Luckily Osmund values his own sleep too much to attack by night, so your parents can work up in the tower with Albert until sunrise.'

He lit one of the torches lying near the armoury door and led Igraine and the Sorrowful Knight across the dark courtyard to the tower. As Igraine stepped on to the bridge a small, furry figure scurried to meet her. Purring, Sisyphus rubbed his head against her knee.

'Oh, Sisyphus!' whispered Igraine, picking up the cat. 'I've missed you so much. Did Albert remember to feed you while I was away?'

'Not enough,' growled Sisyphus, licking the tip of her nose with his rough tongue.

'Your brother is doing splendidly,' said Bertram as he led them up the tower. 'Osmund has been trying all kinds of crafty magic spells, but Albert has foiled them all.'

'Are the Singing Books helping him?' asked Igraine.

'Yes, but they keep on moaning,' said Bertram, 'which Albert really doesn't deserve. Although admittedly the food he conjures up is rather peculiar.'

'There, what did I tell you?' Igraine whispered to the Sorrowful Knight. She nudged Bertram's back. 'What's he been giving you, Bertram? Eggs and biscuits?'

'Buckets full of them!' Bertram groaned, rubbing his fat

paunch. 'I can tell you, the stale bread they threw me down in the Dungeon of Despair was no drier than Albert's biscuits. And as for the eggs! If it was only the shells that came out that colour, but even the yolks are blue.'

With a sigh, he climbed the last few steps and stopped outside the door of the magic workshop. 'That wretched serpent door handle has bitten my hand twice already,' he whispered to Igraine. 'Does it bite you too? Because if not, then . . .'

'That's fine, I'll do it,' Igraine whispered back. 'But keep quiet. I want to give my parents a surprise.'

She put Sisyphus down on the floor, pressed the handle without a sound – the snake just hissed quietly at her touch – and peered around the door into the workshop.

Albert turned his back on her. He was standing at the large table in the middle of the room surrounded by his mice, who were sitting on two six-branched candlesticks dangling their tails. Albert was staring grimly at an empty plate with three Books of Magic standing around it, hands behind their backs, in the position they always adopted when they were going to start singing. Igraine's parents were anxiously resting their snouts on the edge of the table.

'Biscuits and eggs, eggs and biscuits! I don't believe it!' roared Albert, shaking the table so hard that the books stumbled into each other, and one fell right across the plate. Looking cross, it got to its feet again, cast Albert an extremely reproachful glance, and smoothed out its first page. But Albert took no notice. He went on staring gloomily at the empty plate.

'I can send Osmund's own arrows flying back around his ears with a single spell!' he cried. 'But when it comes to something to eat, I can't even manage the simplest soup-making charm! It's enough to drive you crazy!'

Standing at the door, Igraine had to put her hand over her mouth to stop herself giggling.

'Right, here we go. Last try!' growled Albert. 'Careful, books, concentrate!'

He raised his hands in the air.

The Singing Books closed their eyes and began humming quietly.

'Page 223,' said Albert.

Rustling, the books leafed through their pages.

'Apples!' they sang. 'Aaa – aaa – aaapples!' It was a three-part round.

'Apples red, of rosy hue!' called Albert.

'Roo – ooo – ooolls!' sang the books.

'Rolls all brown and crispy too!' said Albert, spinning round on his own axis on the tip of one toe.

'Come hither, come hither, oh do!' sang the books, still in three parts.

'Hither come and fill this plate!' Albert leaped into the air. 'Fill the kitchen, do not wait!'

'Aaaabraaa . . . !' sang the books happily, '. . . braacadaaabrah, fortissimo, pianissimo!'

Then they slammed themselves shut. There was total silence.

Albert had closed his eyes.

'Well, what about it, mice?' he asked impatiently, without opening his eyes again. 'Did it work this time?'

The mice began squeaking excitedly. Albert opened his eyes and leaned over the plate with a happy smile. An apple and a roll lay on it.

'What a wonderfully red apple, my boy!' said Sir Lamorak.

'Yes, and look at that roll!' The Fair Melisande snuffled appreciatively. 'It's a real picture. I never saw a nicer roll. Well done, Albert; well sung, books.'

Flattered, the books took a bow.

Albert picked up the apple, polished it on a corner of his magic coat, and bit into it.

The apple crumbled.

Igraine pressed her hand over her mouth as hard as she could.

'Biscuit crumbs!' roared Albert, slinging the apple out of the window. With a dark look, he reached for the roll. When he broke it in half, blue egg yolk dripped out.

It was too much. Igraine burst out laughing, so loud that the Books of Magic clung to each other in fright.

'Igraine!' said Albert, without turning round. 'My little sister's back.' With a sigh, he gathered up his mice, put them in the pockets of his magic coat, and brushed apple-biscuit crumbs off its collar.

Sir Lamorak and the Fair Melisande, however, ran to their daughter in such excitement that they swept the Books of Magic off the table and almost knocked Albert over in their delight.

'Honey! Did you get the giant's hairs?' cried the Fair Melisande, nuzzling her daughter lovingly with her black snout.

'Yes, of course.' Igraine took the bag containing Garleff's hairs from her belt and handed it to Albert.

'She really got them!' cried the Books of Magic. All of them who were still sitting on the shelves hurried down to join the others. The three books that had helped to conjure up the biscuit crumbs slid down the table legs and hopped excitedly about at Albert's feet.

'Let's have a look, let's have a look!' they cried.

'Well done, little sister,' said Albert, appreciatively pulling Igraine's earlobe. 'I'll soak the hairs at once, so that we can begin working on the spell to change pigs back to parents.'

'Ooh, genuine giant's hairs!' whispered the Books of Magic, clustering around Albert's legs so that he hardly knew where to put his feet down. 'Show us, do show us!'

Albert took Garleff's hairs out of the bag and bent down to show them to the books. 'There you are. But for heaven's sake stop making all that racket.'

'Yes, yes, they really are giant's hairs, red hairs from a

giant!' squealed the books in their shrill little voices. 'Fresh too! Top quality! Thicker than the quill of a feather, red as a fox's coat. Ooh, the magic you can do with those! Come on, come on!' They tugged at Albert's magic coat and hung on to its hem. 'Soak them, soak them! Their power grows less with every passing hour.'

But as they tried to haul Albert off with them, Igraine barred their way. 'Wait a minute!' she said. 'First there's someone I have to introduce to you all!' She turned and led the Sorrowful Knight into the room.

'This,' she said, 'is the Sorrowful Knight of the Mount of Tears. He's a friend of the giant Garleff, and he very kindly escorted me home. And these,' she added, pointing to Albert and the two pigs, 'are my big brother Albert and my parents. My parents don't usually look like that, but I think they're still nice this way, don't you?'

The knight took his helmet off and bowed low to Albert and the two pigs, while the books, full of curiosity, immediately surrounded him.

'A genuine knight, take a look at that, will you?' said one in its reedy voice.

'His armour is rather dented,' whispered another book. 'Almost as bad as the dents old Pelleas got from falling off his horse all the time.'

'That helmet could do with dusting,' commented a third book.

Rather embarrassed, the Sorrowful Knight cleared his throat.

'Shut up, will you?' said Igraine, so angrily that the books flinched away. 'We haven't been sitting around on a nice upholstered shelf like you. We've rescued a dragon, fought the One-Eyed Duke and outwitted Osmund's guards.'

'Oh, dear me!' groaned the Fair Melisande. 'That sounds terrible, honey. And I am very grateful indeed to this noble knight for seeing you safely home.'

'Yes, to be sure,' snorted Sir Lamorak, pricking up his piggy ears. 'That was very kind of you, Sir Sorrowful Knight of . . . er, the Mount of Tears.'

The Sorrowful Knight bowed again. 'It was an honour,' he replied. 'And a pleasure. Your daughter is brave and fearless, and of a most chivalrous cast of mind, even if she and I sometimes don't see the rules of chivalry in quite the same way.'

Pleased, Lamorak and Melisande lowered their snouts. 'My dear . . . er, Sorrowful Knight, it makes us very happy to hear that,' said Sir Lamorak, much moved.

Igraine deeply regretted having taken her helmet off because now, unfortunately, everyone could see her blushing to the roots of her hair. 'Bertram told me that Albert's been foiling all Osmund's magic tricks,' she quickly said.

Albert's expression was one of deliberate modesty. 'Well,

admittedly I didn't do badly,' he said.

'How about the food?' Igraine couldn't resist. Albert was looking so terribly self-satisfied.

'Yes, all right, I still have to work on that a bit,' he muttered. 'But now I'm going to grate the hairs and then soak them.'

'Use the condensed dragon's vapour, my boy!' Sir Lamorak called after him. 'It works even better than water-snake saliva. I think we still have a small jar left.'

The books followed Albert in a long procession as he disappeared into the back room of the workshop – the stirring and boiling room, as Igraine called it.

Her father put his pink front trotters up on the window sill and looked out at the night. 'I'm really looking forward to turning that Osmund into a shape that suits him better,' he said. 'What do you think, honey, would a cockroach fit the bill, or would one of those fish that wallow in the mud be better?'

'I'll have to think about that,' said Igraine. 'But first I want to hear what's been going on here while I was away.'

'Oh, nothing much,' replied her mother, nudging her lovingly with her snout. 'Osmund is a terrible bore with his threats and his rather second-rate magic, and he's spoiling our view with all those tents. The noise is rather a nuisance at times too. Yesterday he tried making the castle fall down by rather inexpertly casting an earthquake spell. The tower wobbled a bit, and four gargoyles lost their noses, but otherwise nothing happened. The man's a fool. He'd do terrible damage with our books.'

'He certainly would,' agreed Sir Lamorak. 'And your brother is acquitting himself bravely, but it's high time we got our own magic powers back so that we can put an end to all this tail-curling nonsense.'

'I'm really sorry that you are our guest at Pimpernel at such a difficult time,' Melisande continued to the Sorrowful Knight, who was still standing by the door looking uncertain of himself. 'This is a small castle, but we always have a couple of rooms ready for unexpected guests. So if you'd like to stay in spite of the racket that man Osmund is kicking up . . .'

'My thanks to you,' said the Sorrowful Knight. 'I would be happy to stay. But if you will allow me to, I'll sleep up on the wall behind the battlements. Only under the stars am I free from my sorrowful dreams.'

'Well, just as you like,' said the Fair Melisande, looking thoughtfully at the knight. 'But my special tea is good for sorrowful dreams too. I'll ask one of the books to take a mug of it up to you on the wall, with a plate of Albert's biscuits. Although,' she added, giving the knight an enchanting piggy smile, 'they really are rather dry even for my palate, piggy as it is at present.'

THE BATTLE OF
THE MAGICIANS

Osmund attacked the next morning as soon as the sun had risen. Igraine fell out of bed in alarm when the noise started. Sleepy, and still feeling grubby from her journey, she clambered into her armour, gave Sisyphus his milk in the kitchen and then went out into the courtyard. Albert and the Sorrowful Knight were already up on the battlements.

'The moat will be brimming over with fish if any more of Osmund's half-witted knights fall in,' said Albert, as Igraine pushed in between them.

She looked anxiously down at the moat. 'Oh, dear. Sisyphus can't tell real fish from knight-fish,' she said. 'And what else is he going to eat? We don't have much choice for him. Except those mice, of course.'

'Just let him try it!' said Albert menacingly. 'That cat's too fat anyway. Give him biscuits. After all, that's what we're eating ourselves. Though Bertram is in the kitchen at this very minute trying to rustle up something else.'

The tents outside the castle were turning red in the light of the rising sun. The bank of the moat was swarming with archers, catapults, and soldiers trying to build wooden bridges across the water. The gargoyles smacked their lips and belched as they swallowed fiery arrows and iron cannonballs. The stone lions crouched above the gateway, roaring and using their paws to deflect any missiles that flew their way.

'This whole thing is getting monotonous,' sighed Albert, settling down between two crenellations. He took a small Book of Magic out of his coat pocket and placed it on his lap. It began humming quietly.

Down below, some of Osmund's men were loading up the great catapults with bundles of burning brushwood. Albert looked at them, shaking his head.

'Take a look at that, will you?' he said. 'They're trying to smoke us out now. I call it really clever to go burning a castle down when you want to steal the books in it. A brainwave.' He wrinkled his nose in derision. 'Page 23,' he told the book, 'and then page 77 right after that.'

The little Book of Magic opened itself and warbled a tune that sounded very much like 'Twinkle, twinkle, little star'. Albert turned up the sleeves of his magic coat, and was just in time to catch two mice that fell out. 'Didn't I tell you to stay in the magic workshop?' he scolded, as he put them back in his pocket. Then he raised his hands in the air.

As Osmund's men prepared to fire the catapults, Albert scrutinized them with disdain, snapped his fingers, and called:

> *'Little birds fly round about!*
> *All the flames will fizzle out.*
> *Mix with Albert and his magic*
> *And the ending will be tragic.*
> *Your fingers you will burn today*
> *As you turn to run away.'*

The bundles of brushwood exploded with a mighty bang, and the wheels dropped off the catapults and rolled away at top speed. Fountains of coloured light shot high in the air, sparks fell into the water lilies and rained down on Osmund's men. Cursing, they ran about in confusion to get away from the jets of fire. But the knights commanding them drove the men back to the moat with their swords and made them scoop up water to put out the flames.

'Who cares if they bale out the whole moat?' said Albert, as the Book of Magic shut itself with a self-satisfied sigh. 'Those catapults are finished. I wrecked half a dozen others yesterday. Look at those fools slopping water all over their hands. They'll have webbed fingers by noon.' He turned to Igraine and the Sorrowful Knight with a pleased smile. 'How did you like my firework show? First-rate magic, wasn't it?'

136

'Yes, definitely first-rate,' Igraine agreed. 'But you'd better take a look down there now. They've nearly finished building their wooden bridges.'

'So they have. Busy, busy little bees,' commented Albert, looking bored. 'Why don't you call in the snakes to deal with that, little sister? They're happier to obey you than me. Hey, what's going on there?' He snapped his fingers, and a hail of burning arrows shot by Osmund's archers to set fire to the drawbridge turned above the moat in an elegant curve. Albert snapped his fingers a second time, and the arrows hissed back towards the startled archers, leaving a fiery tail behind them. Terrified, the men raised their shields, but the arrows buzzed around them like giant dragonflies all aflame, and attacked the archers from behind. Soon every arrow was chasing an archer through the camp.

Igraine would have loved to watch the rest of the show, but Albert was right – it was time to call in the snakes. Presumably they were down on the bed of the moat, hiding from the unaccustomed noise that Osmund's men were kicking up, but Igraine knew they would hear her all the same. A sharp hiss through her teeth, a dozen of Albert's biscuits, and next moment the water around the water lilies was rippling, and three snakes raised their heads from the moat.

Osmund's soldiers were so busy laying their footbridges across the enchanted water that they never even noticed the snakes. But the snakes had noticed them. They shot through the water, hissing angrily, coiled round the bridges, and squeezed them until the wood splintered. Five bridge-builders fell into the moat in their fright, adding a few more fish to it.

Igraine shook her head at their clumsiness. 'I thought this man Osmund could work magic?' she enquired. 'We haven't seen much of that yet. Oh, my word, Sisyphus!' she exclaimed, as the tomcat dropped a long fishbone in her lap, shimmering and suspiciously silvery. 'Have you gone and eaten another of those knight-fish? I'm afraid I'll have to shut you in somewhere.'

Sisyphus showed his contempt by catching a buzzing fly and consuming it with a loud smack of his lips.

'Oh, let him alone.' Albert came to his help, shooing his mice back as they raised their heads from his coat pocket

and stuck their tiny tongues out at Sisyphus. 'That's all the knights deserve!'

But the Sorrowful Knight shook his head. 'Show mercy to the men down below, noble Albert,' he said. 'I know they have designs on your life and the lives of your family, but many of them aren't doing it of their own free will. Osmund's knights have dragged them away from their fields and their homes and brought them here. Where else would all these soldiers come from? Half of them probably don't even know why Osmund is laying siege to Pimpernel.'

'Did you hear that, Sisyphus?' Igraine turned to her sulky cat with a stern expression. 'No more of those silver fish, however good they taste. Otherwise I'll let Albert turn you into a dog after all.'

'We're not friends any more,' growled the tomcat.

'But I'd turn you into a nice dog, Sisyphus,' said Albert, feeding the mice in his pocket with a few biscuit crumbs. 'Osmund could never do that. His magic powers really aren't anything special. Yesterday he was trying harder than today, but some spells don't even occur to him. Even if he had the books, our friend Osmund would never be a great magician. I'd say he's passed Grade Five at the very most.' And with a conspiratorial smile, he bent down to the little Book of Magic which sat sleepily on his lap, blinking as the sun slowly rose higher in the sky. 'We showed him some real magic between us, right?'

Flattered, the book chuckled and stroked its own pages.

'Noble Albert, would that be Osmund over there?' asked the Sorrowful Knight, pointing to a figure down among the tents.

'You're right, it is!' replied Albert. 'Let's see what he has to offer now.'

Two servants carried the new master of Darkrock up to the moat in an upholstered armchair, and put it down beside the water.

'Shall I fetch Mama and Papa?' asked Igraine, trying not to show that Osmund's look of determination made her a little anxious after all.

But Albert shook his head. 'No, no, I can deal with this on my own. They're preparing the magic to change themselves back, so we don't want to disturb them, or we might have piggy parents for the rest of our lives.'

'All right, have it your own way,' murmured Igraine, while Osmund slowly and deliberately rose from his chair. The archers lowered their bows. The new catapults that had been wheeled up stopped, and all the soldiers looked at their lord and master. An eerie silence fell over Pimpernel Castle. And when Osmund raised his hands in the air, Igraine saw that he had blackened his palms with soot.

'Ah, sooty hands,' whispered Albert. 'I think I know what spell he's going to try. Page 637, book. Quick.'

The little Book of Magic hastily began leafing through its pages.

Down by the moat Osmund closed his eyes, raising his blackened hands a little higher, and called in a menacing voice:

> 'Rotten bridge, come down for me,
> To my will obedient be!
> Recognize that my black heart
> Now commands the magic art.
> Lie down, bridge, obey you must,
> Or you will burn to ash and dust.'

The stone lions bared their teeth and roared angrily down at him. The gargoyles made faces. But the hinges of the drawbridge squealed – and slowly it began to lower itself towards the moat.

Osmund's men waved their swords jubilantly in the air.

'Albert, do something!' cried Igraine in alarm. 'Quick.'

'Yes, all right!' called Albert back. 'Have you found that page yet, book?'

'It's stuck!' wailed the book, leafing through its pages with trembling fingers. 'There must be jam on it.'

'Jam?' thundered Albert. 'Haven't we always forbidden you books to snack on jam or anything else sticky?' He roughly picked up the book and tried to separate the pages that were stuck together.

But the drawbridge went on lowering itself.

Osmund looked up at Albert with a mocking smile. His soldiers gathered behind the chair, ready to charge over the faithless bridge and into the castle.

'I'll have it in a minute!' cried Albert, fiddling frantically with the little book. 'It won't take more than a few seconds.'

'Come with me, noble Igraine!' cried the Sorrowful Knight, and in his clanking armour he raced to the flight of steps leading down to the courtyard. 'We must block the chain!' he called to her. 'Fetch lances, spears, anything.'

Igraine nodded, and ran to the armoury so fast that she stumbled over her own feet.

Meanwhile, the Sorrowful Knight braced his weight against the crank that worked the drawbridge. It was moving as if a ghostly hand were turning it. He tried desperately to turn it back the other way, but Osmund's magic was too strong, and however hard the Sorrowful Knight tried the bridge went on coming down – more slowly, to be sure, but it was still lowering itself. And when he finally stuck his sword into one of the links in the chain, the point of the sword broke off.

'Here, take these!' cried Igraine, throwing him all the lances she had been able to find in her haste. They thrust their shafts through the iron links of the chain one by one to stop it moving, but lance after lance splintered – and still the bridge was coming down. There was already a gap showing in the wall, and soon only the wood of the gate would protect the castle.

But suddenly Igraine heard a shrill chanting from the battlements, and the next moment Albert's voice rang out loud and clear:

> *'Faithless bridge, rise up, rise high,*
> *Or I'll turn you to a fly.*
> *I'll feed you to the birds of prey,*
> *As driftwood you will float away.*
> *I'm warning you,*
> *Don't anger me,*
> *Or furious as a bull I'll be.'*

Osmund's men groaned. The bridge stopped, swinging on its rusty chains – and refused to move an inch further down.

Osmund ranted.

Osmund raged.

He stamped his feet, smeared the soot from his hands all over his face in his fury, and threw first his armchair and then his servants into the moat. The bridge still didn't budge.

Spell after magic spell Osmund cast on the castle, but they all bounced off like clods of earth thrown by a child against a knight's shield.

Meanwhile Igraine and the Sorrowful Knight clung to the crank, not daring to let go of it. Only when Albert signalled to them from the battlements did they cautiously, very cautiously, raise the drawbridge again.

Igraine's legs were still trembling when they were standing behind the battlements again.

Sisyphus padded to meet her and rubbed his head against her knee.

'Oh, so we're friends again after all, are we?' she asked.

'Friends,' purred Sisyphus, stalking away with his tail upright in the air.

'Keep away from that moat!' Igraine called after him, but the cat had already vanished down the steps.

'He's always slinking off to the little gate down there in the wall,' said Albert. 'One nudge of his nose, and it's so rotten it opens at once. Well, how do you think we did, little sister?' He leaned casually back against the battlements with the Book of Magic on his shoulder. They both looked very pleased with themselves and the world in general.

'It was terrific,' replied Igraine, peering over the wall. 'Apart from the jam, that is.'

Osmund had disappeared, like his chair.

'Strawberry jam!' Albert sighed. 'Those books have been forbidden to touch jam for at least a hundred years, but they're crazy for anything sweet and sticky.'

The little book cleared its throat with an embarrassed sound, wiped some dust off its cover and looked the other way.

'May I ask you a question, noble Albert?' said the Sorrowful Knight. Out by the moat, Osmund's men were rolling heavy rocks up to the few catapults that were still working. The attackers weren't giving up in a hurry.

'Of course. What is it?' Albert replied.

The knight hesitated for a moment. Then he asked, 'Where is Rowan Heartless? Your sister told me that he is Osmund's castellan.'

'Oh, you mean the Iron Hedgehog.' Albert sat down on the wall again. The little Book of Magic hummed, Albert rubbed his hands together and the rocks in the catapults turned into tiny dragons fluttering swiftly away. 'He rode off this morning with a few soldiers, probably to steal pigs and chickens from the peasants in the nearest village so that Osmund can feed his army. He wasn't outside the castle yesterday morning either; he didn't turn up until around midday.'

'Ah,' murmured the Sorrowful Knight, and he gazed into the distance, lost in thought.

Igraine looked sideways at him, rather worried.

'Coming with me?' she asked, to give him something else to think about. 'I'd like to see how my parents are getting on with the magic that's supposed to turn them into humans again.'

The Sorrowful Knight looked at Albert. 'Do you need my help?'

'No, no, off you go,' said Albert. 'I'm doing fine on my own. Osmund will sulk for a while now. He always does when his spells don't work. But send me up a few biscuits. And by the way, little sister,' he added, 'your cat has just caught three more fish in the moat. Very silvery fish. He's sitting outside the little gate.'

A NOBLE OFFER

ir Lamorak and the Fair Melisande were stirring
something with sticks in a large cauldron when
Igraine and the Sorrowful Knight entered the magic
workshop.

'I think we need a little more angelica, my love,'
mumbled Sir Lamorak. The stick he was holding in his
snout almost slipped out as he spoke.

'More angelica? Yes, you could be right.' The Fair
Melisande turned to the books, which were playing hide
and seek under the table. 'Would one of you be kind
enough to fetch us a pinch of powdered angelica?'

Grumbling, the smallest book set off for the next room.

'Well, how's it going?' asked Igraine. 'When will the
magic potion be ready?'

'Potion? Oh, goodness me, we don't drink it, honey!'
replied Melisande. 'We just have to take a bath in it,
understand? The giant's hairs have dissolved nicely. Now
the whole thing has to steep in a magic vessel for six hours,

and then we pour it into a tub down in the bath-house and mix it with warm water. I think we'll be ready to start turning back into human form as soon as the sun sets.'

'Yes, and by midnight at the latest we'll have turned that Osmund into the nastiest creature we can think of,' said Sir Lamorak. 'What's the wretch doing now?'

'Oh, Albert has everything in hand,' said Igraine. She didn't mention the drawbridge and the strawberry jam. Her parents had enough worries of their own.

'Did Albert tell you there could be a little problem while we take the magic bath?' asked her mother.

The book came back with the angelica, climbed up on Melisande's bristly back, and tipped the powder into the ginger-coloured brew. A delicious smell rose to all their noses.

'Another problem?' asked Igraine anxiously.

'I'm afraid so, my dear.' Sir Lamorak gave the brew another good stir and then threw his stick into the corner. 'This transformation will need all the magic power available at Pimpernel. So your mother and I are afraid that our defences – er – won't be operating at full strength while we're taking the magic bath. Do you see what I mean?'

Igraine frowned. 'You mean the gargoyles, the lions, the water snakes, the magic spell on the moat . . .'

'. . . will be out of action.' Her father finished the sentence for her. 'So to speak.'

This was clearly bad news. Very bad news. 'Then Albert

is going to have his hands full,' murmured Igraine. 'How will he manage? He can't be everywhere at once. How long will it take your magic bath to work?'

'About an hour,' replied Sir Lamorak. 'If none of the books fall in. If they do it will take a bit longer. They're rather clumsy sometimes.'

'An hour!' Worried, Igraine went to the window and looked out. The sky had clouded over. It was raining. But Osmund's soldiers were still bombarding Pimpernel with arrows, fire and stones. They had already built new wooden footbridges for crossing the moat, and now they were making rafts and trying to shoot ropes with iron hooks attached up to the battlements. There was only too good a view of all this from the tower. Igraine even saw horses pulling a mighty battering ram towards the castle. Although several men were urging them on, they were making slow progress, but at some time or other they would reach the moat. Were they planning to break down the castle walls with the battering ram, or make a hole in the drawbridge? More work for Albert, thought Igraine, turning her back to the window. A gloomy silence filled the workshop.

Until the Sorrowful Knight cleared his throat.

'When exactly do you mean to work your shape-changing magic?' he asked the two pigs.

'We can get into the tub at sunset,' replied the Fair Melisande. 'Osmund usually stops attacking about then, but he'll probably notice that our magical defences are down, because I am sorry to say that the gargoyles snore heavily when they fall into a deep sleep of that kind, and the lions don't look very terrifying either.'

The Sorrowful Knight nodded. 'Very well,' he said. 'Then there's only one way to make sure that you are undisturbed. I will challenge Rowan Heartless, whom you call the Spiky Knight, to single combat at sunset. I am sure Osmund will pause in his attack on your castle while his castellan takes up my challenge. And his soldiers will want to watch us too. No one will notice that Pimpernel is almost undefended, and you can regain your proper shapes without any danger that the castle will be captured.'

What on earth was he talking about?

'But you said you couldn't defeat him!' cried Igraine. 'You said you feared him more than anything in the world! No! Pimpernel is our castle, so . . .' Igraine looked as determined as she possibly could, '. . . so I'll distract Osmund's attention by challenging the Spiky Knight myself.'

'You, honey?' squealed her horrified parents.

But the Sorrowful Knight put his hand on her shoulder and looked at her gravely, much too gravely for her liking.

'Noble Igraine,' he said. 'Your fearless heart does you great credit. But sometimes fearlessness is not a good counsellor. You must learn to fear some things, and to judge your own strength properly. A girl of twelve, however brave, cannot possibly face a battle-hardened knight like Rowan in combat. He will hold you up to derision and tread your pride in the dust. No. I will fight the Spiky Knight – if he accepts my challenge. I only hope I can keep him occupied a little longer than I did at our last meetings. But at least I am a fit and proper opponent for him. Can you understand that?'

Igraine bent her head and wiped some dove droppings off her armour. 'Yes, I'm afraid so,' she muttered. 'But I'm worried about you.'

That made the Sorrowful Knight smile. 'There's no need, believe me. Rowan Heartless takes no pleasure in killing his opponents. He prefers to humiliate them again and again. And he wouldn't want to deprive himself of that pleasure by killing me, do you see?'

Igraine nodded.

'Good. Then let us return to your brother on the wall and see if Rowan has come back yet, shall we?'

'Er . . . noble Knight of . . . er, the Mount of Tears!' Sir Lamorak cleared his throat several times. 'I thank you heartily for your unselfish offer. And I . . . er . . . hope we can do you a similar great service when we have our magic powers back, don't you agree, my love?'

The Fair Melisande bowed her bristly head. 'There are no words for the gratitude we owe you, sir!' she said.

'Don't mention it!' replied the Sorrowful Knight, returning her bow.

'Well, come along then, books!' Sir Lamorak turned. 'Time to pour the concoction into the magic vessel.'

The books rolled up their sleeves, gathered around the tub, and raised it from the floor. Then, panting and gasping, they carried it into the next room.

'It only works if the Books of Magic pour the concoction into the vessel with their own hands,' Sir Lamorak whispered to the Sorrowful Knight. 'They usually spill quite a bit, and they hate physical work too, but this particular spell demands it.'

Side by side, the two pigs trotted after the groaning books. In the doorway, Melisande turned once more. 'Oh, Igraine,' she said, 'could you send Albert up to us as soon as he's free? He has to make it snow in the next room so that the concoction will cool down more quickly.'

'Yes, of course,' said Igraine, but she could think of only one thing. The Sorrowful Knight was determined to fight Rowan Heartless.

ALBERT'S PLAN

Albert made it snow in the magic workshop, of course. That wasn't a particularly complicated spell. But as he returned to the walls he was looking anxious.

'What's this they're telling me?' he said to the Sorrowful Knight. 'Are you really planning to challenge Osmund's castellan to distract them? It's not a bad idea, but if it's to work there's something we must take care of before the fight.'

'What kind of something would that be?' asked Bertram, putting a large pan of fried fish down on the battlements.

'Are you sure these fish never walked on two legs?' asked Igraine.

'Sure,' replied Bertram.

Albert looked at the gigantic battering ram that had just been manoeuvred into position on the bank of the moat. 'One of us,' he said, taking a piece of fish, 'must steal into the Spiky Knight's tent.'

Bertram almost swallowed a bone the wrong way. 'This is no time for joking, Albert,' he said. 'You've been eating too many of your horrible biscuits.'

'I'm not joking.' Albert leaned over the wall, clapped his hands three times, and hummed a note that sounded horribly out of tune. All at once the iron head of the battering ram slumped forward and dropped into the moat. 'Easy-peasy!' murmured Albert. He snapped his fingers to send back a quiverful of burning arrows that had lost their way, and turned to the Sorrowful Knight. 'Your fight with the Iron Hedgehog,' he said, 'has to keep Osmund occupied for a full hour. That's a long time. If he unhorses you during the first tilt, you'll be risking your neck for nothing.'

'What are you talking about?' cried Igraine indignantly. 'The Knight of the Mount of Tears is a wonderful knight! He knows better than anyone how to—'

The Sorrowful Knight raised his hand. 'Let your brother finish, Igraine,' he said.

'However wonderful a knight he may be,' Albert went on, 'he doesn't stand a chance. The Iron Hedgehog always wins. When he's jousting with a lance he unhorses all his opponents at the first tilt. I'm right, aren't I?'

The Sorrowful Knight bowed his head. 'Your brother is indeed right, noble Igraine,' he said quietly. 'As you know, it's happened to me three times already.'

'I thought as much.' Albert nodded in a satisfied way.

'Did you never wonder why?'

The knight looked enquiringly at him. 'What do you mean?'

'The Iron Hedgehog uses magic, of course!' cried Albert. 'It's as clear as day!'

'What are you saying?' Incredulously, the Sorrowful Knight shook his head. 'That can't be true!'

'I tell you, he wins by magic!' Albert repeated. 'Ask Bertram.'

'Albert's right.' The Master of Horse threw a few fishbones over the castle walls. 'Back at Darkrock, I overheard Osmund's servants talking. One of them was saying that Osmund had cast a spell on Heartless's jousting lance in gratitude for his faithful services. That's why the Hedgehog always uses the same lance for his first tilt.'

The Sorrowful Knight was looking as if someone had hit him hard on his helmet. 'But that's impossible!' he stammered. 'To use magic is against the honour of a knight!'

'The honour of a knight my foot!' Albert laughed derisively. 'The Hedgehog couldn't care less about such things. He wants to be unbeatable, and with an enchanted lance he is. I bet you it glows green. That's the way you can always recognize weapons with a victory spell on them. So the fact is, if your challenge is supposed to give us a breathing space, the spell on the lance must be broken.

It's not all that difficult, but one of us will have to creep into Osmund's camp to do it. And unfortunately I can't, because we never know when Osmund will mount his next magic attack, so—'

'So I'll go,' said Igraine.

'That's what I thought, little sister!' Albert gave her a broad smile. 'But you must hurry. The sun is high in the sky, and I'm sure Heartless will soon be back. Come on. I'll give you something I found in the armoury.'

Igraine stood up, but the Sorrowful Knight took her arm. 'No. This is out of the question!' he said. 'I will be the one to go, of course.'

'No, let me do it,' said Bertram, putting the knight aside. 'You fight the Iron Hedgehog, I'll steal into his tent and make sure you have a fair chance.'

'Oh, stop talking nonsense!' said Albert, impatiently interrupting. 'Neither of you knows the first thing about magic! Igraine may not know much either, but at least she's grown up among magicians! She's the one who must go. But Bertram can accompany her as a watchdog.'

Bertram bowed to Igraine with a broad grin. 'Your faithful watchdog at your service, noble lady!'

'This is madness!' cried the Sorrowful Knight. 'They'll both be found and captured.'

'Oh no, I don't think so,' said Albert mysteriously.

Igraine had been sure she knew every single item in the

armoury of Pimpernel Castle, every shield, every sword, even every cloak, however moth-eaten. But she had never before noticed the strange thing that Albert took out of a small chest. It looked like a veil, except that the fabric was covered with scales, transparent scales fitting closely together.

'As you know, I never usually come here,' said Albert, carefully smoothing out the strange fabric. 'But when Osmund turned up outside the castle with his army I told myself it might be a good idea to find out what our ancestors stored here to defend themselves. And I discovered this.'

'But what is it?' asked Bertram.

'A dragon's skin, of course,' replied Albert. 'Our great-grandfather Pelleas was friends with several dragons. I assume one of them gave it to him as a present. The dragon who shed this skin can't have been more than sixty or seventy years old, so it was still quite small.' Albert reached into the chest again, and took out a second, distinctly larger skin. 'This one ought to fit you, Bertram. The dragon who shed it was a good bit older – perhaps it was the same dragon some time later. I'm sure you know that dragons shed their skins every fourteen years, don't you?'

Igraine shook her head.

Albert threw her the smaller skin. When she caught it, it felt like picking up spun air.

'But what do we do with them?' asked Bertram, baffled.

'They'll make you invisible,' said Albert. 'Try it. Drape them over your heads.'

Igraine and Bertram did as he said – and disappeared. Disappeared without trace.

Pleased with himself, Albert folded his arms.

'I thought those were just a couple of dirty old veils!' gasped the invisible Igraine.

'Well, there you are!' Albert shrugged his shoulders. 'Sometimes big brothers know best, little sister. Now, get down that tunnel of our great-grandfather's. And oh, yes – I almost forgot the most important thing.' He took a small gold container and a box out of his coat pocket. 'Take this with you, Igraine. Dust the point of the enchanted lance with the powder from this container. Then set it alight with a taper from this box, and murmur the Red Chant – which I hope you still know by heart! That will break the strongest victory spell.'

Igraine's hand came out of nowhere, pinched his nose – and stowed the little container and the box away under the dragon skin.

'Watch out for the wind, for branches, for anything that could pluck the dragon skin off your head, understand?' called Albert, as the door of the armoury was opened by what might have been a ghostly hand. 'And remember, you must hurry! If the Hedgehog gets his hands on you, even I can't help you.'

'Don't worry, big brother, we'll do it!' Igraine's voice came back. 'And feed Sisyphus, will you? I shut him up in my room.'

Then the armoury door closed again.

In the Spiky Knight's Tent

Igraine liked being invisible. She enjoyed seeing the foolish expressions on the faces of Osmund's men as she jostled them, and luckily there was such a crowd among the tents that they had forgotten about it next minute. None of them suspected that the daughter of the magicians they were besieging was walking around their camp, unseen. No one stopped Igraine and Bertram. No one swept the dragon skins off their heads and made the invisible spies visible again. And finally they reached Rowan Heartless's red tent. Only a little way off, four knights stood on guard outside Osmund's tent, but the castellan's tent was unguarded.

Igraine glanced back at the castle. She could see no one but Albert standing on the battlements. The gargoyles on the walls were swallowing and chewing, pulling faces and spitting flames over the moat, while the lions struck out with their paws and roared, making the ground shake all the way to the Spiky Knight's tent.

'Are you there, Bertram?' whispered Igraine. The one drawback to invisibility was that while other people couldn't see them, they couldn't see each other either.

'Right in front of you,' Bertram's voice whispered in her ear. 'Let's go in.'

Igraine looked around her one last time, pulled aside the heavy fabric of the tent flap, and slipped underneath.

It was dark and stuffy inside. Through the sides of the tent red light fell on a narrow bed, a table, and richly covered chairs embroidered with the Heartless Knight's coat of arms. Four falcons were chained to a golden perch beside the stand that held his swords. They wore leather hoods covering their eyes, and moved their heads restlessly as Igraine came close to them.

'Hunting falcons!' she whispered. 'The Hedgehog takes his falcons with him even on a siege. But where's his lance?' She looked round for it. The smallest of the birds croaked excitedly and stepped restlessly back and forth on its perch. 'Sssh!' hissed Igraine. 'It's all right.'

'There! Look behind the birds!' whispered Bertram.

'Oh, no!' whispered Igraine. 'He has five lances, Bertram – five!' The smallest falcon spread its wings and opened its hooked beak, but Igraine bravely pushed her way past it. Not even a hundred hairy spiders with their sticky webs could have kept her from the lances now (or so she hoped, anyway).

'Oh, Bertram, how could we have been so stupid?' she

whispered as they stood looking at the lances. 'Of course he has several. Now what? Albert's powder will never be enough for them all!'

'It's the middle one!' whispered Bertram. 'Don't you see its point glowing green? Just as Albert said.'

He was right!

Igraine carefully drew the lance out of its holder, carried it past the squawking, flapping falcon and put it on the table. If you looked closely, you could see the faint green glow quite clearly.

'What a cheat!' she whispered. 'He really does use an enchanted lance.'

She listened for sounds outside. The noises of the camp came through the sides of the tent, but there was nothing unusual to be heard. No footsteps approached, no horse snorted outside the tent entrance. Reassured, Igraine took the dragon skin off her head and opened the little container with Albert's powder inside.

'What are you doing?' whispered Bertram uneasily. 'I can see you.'

Igraine went up to the table and ran her finger over the length of the lance. It was a beautiful weapon, with costly decoration and a wooden shaft as hard as iron. 'I can't disenchant this thing if I can't see my own fingers,' she hissed, as she carefully trickled Albert's powder out of the container and over the point of the lance. It clung to the metal like hoarfrost clinging to a damp leaf. Next Igraine took out Albert's tapers and rubbed one between her fingers. It burst into flame with a sharp hiss. Igraine let the white flame lick up the powder and began to whisper the Red Chant – one of the ninety-nine magic spells that every magician's child must learn (even if she wants to be a knight):

> 'Be you gone, you magic shimmer,
> May your light grow ever dimmer.
> Lance thrown by a wicked arm . . .'

She rubbed her forehead. How did it go on?

'Igraine?' Bertram's voice sounded very anxious.

'Don't worry. I'll remember in a minute!' Igraine whispered. 'Lance thrown by a wicked arm . . . oh, yes!' She raised her hands, and heard Bertram heave a sigh of relief:

> 'Doing honest knights such harm,
> Now for ever be you free
> Of magic and of treachery.'

She had hardly spoken the last word when the white flame went out – and took the green glow with it.

'Won't he notice?' Bertram too had taken the dragon

skin off his head, which made him invisible only from the
shoulders down – quite a strange sight, but it was terribly
stuffy under those skins.

Igraine shrugged, and took the lance back to its place.
Once again the fourth falcon spread its wings, but the
others perched there as if they were asleep.

'I hope
not,' said
Igraine,
carefully
putting the
weapon back in its
holder. 'But even
if he does notice, a
victory spell like
that can't be worked
again in a hurry. At
least this evening
he can't use a magic
lance, that's for
sure.'

She quickly drew
the dragon skin over her
head again and tiptoed to
the entrance of the
tent. Cautiously, she

peered past the flap, looked left, then right – and saw Rowan Heartless riding straight towards her.

He was kicking anyone who came too close to him out of his way. Then he reined his horse in outside Osmund's tent and dismounted with a clink of armour. One of Osmund's servants hurried up and took the reins of the sweating beast.

'Bertram, quick, pull that dragon skin over your head!' hissed Igraine over her shoulder. 'The Hedgehog's back!' Then she peered out again. The Spiky Knight looked round, and disappeared into Osmund's tent.

'Do we have time to escape?' whispered Bertram.

'Yes, he's gone into Osmund's tent,' Igraine whispered back. 'Quick!' She felt Bertram hurry past her into the open air, and was just about to follow him when something occurred to her. In alarm, she looked round. Yes, there was Albert's container still lying on the table, open and empty.

She quickly ran back, hiding under the dragon skin. 'The lid!' she murmured. 'Where's the lid?' She knelt down, looked under the table – and heard footsteps. Clinking footsteps coming closer. A horse neighed.

'What the devil's got into the horse?' she heard Rowan Heartless ask in his cold voice.

'I don't know, sir!' someone anxiously replied. 'He's shying as if he'd seen a ghost.'

The horse neighed again.

Bertram, thought Igraine. The horse can sense Bertram. Let's hope it doesn't kick him in the head. She leaped to her feet and ran for the entrance to the tent. But before she could slip out the Spiky Knight put back the tent flap. Igraine felt his breath on her face, but he looked straight through her. Soundlessly, feeling weak at the knees, she stepped aside, thankful to Albert and her parents for using their magic to make her a suit of armour that didn't clink. Rowan Heartless strode past her and dropped into a chair, stretching his legs out stiffly. 'Squire!' he bellowed.

A weedy boy scurried into the tent, head hunched between his shoulders.

'Take my greaves off and polish them!' growled Heartless. 'And better than you did last time, or I'll have you thrown into that enchanted moat, understand?'

'Yes, sir!' breathed the boy, and set to work.

Igraine began to creep towards the tent's entrance yet again.

'And where's my dinner?' Heartless pounded the table with his fist. Igraine jumped, not daring to move. Three more squires hurried into the tent with dishes and plates, barring her way. She felt like cursing out loud. The horse outside had calmed down. Was Bertram back in the castle yet? Would he be able to open the stone lion's mouth by himself? She had told him what to do and say, but the Master of Horse had never worked magic before. The servants brought the Spiky Knight something to drink,

soldiers complained that they were running out of arrows.
A knight reported the loss of the great battering ram to
one of Albert's diabolical spells. And as Igraine stood
there, waiting for an opportunity to slip out of the tent,
she suddenly saw the lid of the powder container. It was
lying right underneath the falcons' perch, where anyone
could see it clearly. Should she creep over and retrieve
it? She was still invisible. But just as she was about to try,
Rowan the Heartless called for his squire again.

'Did you feed the falcons?' he snapped.

'They wouldn't eat those mice,' replied the squire, not
daring to look at his master.

'What did you say?' The Spiky Knight angrily got to his
feet and went over to the birds. The tip of his shoe nudged
the golden lid aside. In her fright, Igraine bit her lips until
they were almost bleeding.

'You haven't been giving them fruit and vegetables again,
have you?' growled Rowan the Heartless.

The squire's head bent even lower.

'Those falcons are carnivores,' said his master in a
menacingly quiet voice. 'Meat-eaters, hunters, birds of
prey. If you feed them anything but mice once more,' he
said, treading right on the lid, 'I'll tell Osmund to turn
you into a mouse, and perhaps the falcons will like *you*.
Understood?'

'Understood, sir!' breathed the squire.

'Then go and get . . . what the devil's this?' Heartless

raised his foot and picked up the shining lid. 'Feeding the birds out of golden boxes now, are you?'

'I . . . I don't know, sir,' stammered the squire. 'No, sir, no, I really haven't. I was just . . .'

Rowan Heartless examined the lid. He even smelled it. 'Strange,' he murmured suspiciously.

It was high time to get out of there – more than high time. Quietly as a cat, Igraine was tiptoeing towards the tent flap when there was a strange noise outside. It sounded like a hoarse trumpet.

'Go and find out what's up!' Rowan Heartless snapped at his squire. The boy shot past Igraine and out of the tent like lightning.

'Sir, there – there – there's a strange knight on the castle battlements!' he stammered when he stumbled back in again.

'What kind of strange knight?' growled Heartless, standing up.

Igraine's heart beat faster.

'He – he – he's challenging you to single combat!' stuttered the boy.

His master pushed him aside and marched out of the tent. Igraine waited for only a split second. Then she followed him.

The Challenge

Everyone streamed out to the moat, and Igraine let the crowd sweep her along, not that there was anything else she could do. She clutched the dragon skin tightly in case it slipped off in the general turmoil, made her way past the shying horses and walked through a throng of baffled soldiers who stared straight through her. When she reached the moat she stopped behind a catapult. Rowan Heartless was only a few paces away, surrounded by his squires and looking up at the battlements of Pimpernel Castle.

There stood the Sorrowful Knight, without his helmet on and without his shield. Bertram was peering over the wall beside him. So he had made it into the tunnel. He was holding a horn that had been lying around gathering dust in the armoury for years. That was probably what Igraine had heard in the Spiky Knight's tent. She would have loved to wave to the two of them, but among so many enemies she didn't even dare to bring a hand out from under the dragon skin.

'Is that one of the two mysterious knights who slipped through the guards' fingers in the wood?' Igraine heard Heartless ask. 'Devil knows he doesn't look as huge and terrible as they claimed.'

The crowd parted behind him, and Osmund's servants put their master's armchair down beside the castellan. Water was still dripping from the red upholstery. Three men had turned into fish as they hauled it out of the moat.

'What's all this?' asked Osmund in astonishment when he saw the Sorrowful Knight up on the battlements. 'How did that knight get into the castle?'

'He's done what we've been trying to do for days,' replied Rowan Heartless, never taking his eyes off his challenger. 'The guards told me about a fight on the outskirts of the forest last night. It seems that the huge stone lion there came to life and swallowed up two knights.'

Angrily, Osmund turned to his men. 'Have everyone who was on guard in the forest last night thrown into the enchanted moat,' he ordered. 'At once!'

The six guards had no time to run away. They were dragged to the moat and pushed in – and next moment, covered in silvery scales, they were diving down among the water lilies.

'Rowan Heartless, now castellan to Osmund the Greedy, hear me!' the Sorrowful Knight called down from the battlements. 'I, the Sorrowful Knight of the Mount of Tears, challenge you to single combat. When the sun touches the treetops of the wood, I will cross lances with you outside the walls of this castle that your rapacious army is besieging.'

Igraine looked round. Everyone was staring up at the strange knight who dared to challenge Osmund's invincible castellan. This was her moment. It was too far to get to the escape route along the tunnel. She decided to swim the moat.

'So you want to fight me?' Rowan Heartless called up to his challenger. 'Why not? This siege is very tedious and boring. I've no objection to a passage at arms with my jousting lance. And there won't be more than one, unless you've learned to joust better since I last defeated you. Don't think I didn't recognize you, Sorrowful Knight! Why did you creep into this castle by the back door? To play nursemaid to that jug-eared, snotty-nosed beanpole of a boy and his little sister in her silly suit of armour?'

That horrible, horrible, horrible Hedgehog! Perhaps she ought to drag him into the moat with her! Igraine was quivering with rage, but Albert had taught her how to control her anger. 'Sissle-sassle-Pimpernel, hush, red anger, now be still,' she whispered, and her heartbeat slowed down; her head could think again. Back to the castle, Igraine, she thought, slipping past the catapult and making for the moat.

'A knight does not fight with insults, Heartless!' called

the Sorrowful Knight. 'I want your word of knightly honour that if I defeat you your disgraceful master Osmund will raise the siege and leave with all his soldiers.'

'You have my word of honour!' replied Osmund instead of his castellan, but his mocking smile said more clearly than any words what he thought of the strange knight's chances of victory.

'Very well, that's settled!' Rowan Heartless called to his challenger. 'But what's my reward if I defeat you? Will these badly behaved brats finally hand over the Singing Books?'

'Never!' cried Albert, jumping up on the wall beside the Sorrowful Knight. 'Those books have been entrusted to our family for more than three hundred years. The Queen of the Wood-Sprites herself gave them into our care.'

Keep on talking, Albert, thought Igraine, you do it brilliantly. Distract their attention, just for a moment. And she jumped into the moat.

'Something's fallen into the water, sir!' she heard one of Osmund's soldiers calling.

'One of you blockheads, I expect,' replied Osmund without turning round. He was still looking up at Albert.

'Yes, you heard me, Osmund!' Albert called. 'The wood-sprites themselves made the books. Their pages would wither like autumn leaves in your greedy fingers. They'd never sing their spells for you. Never. Not if you live to be as old as our castle. So raise this stupid siege of yours!'

The water in the moat had no effect on Igraine; it didn't harm any member of her family. She need not fear the water snakes either, far from it. They had taught her to swim almost before she could walk, and as for her armour, the Books of Magic hadn't been exaggerating. It really was waterproof. But the dragon skin kept almost drifting away from her, and that made swimming hard work.

I know, she thought, why don't I ask the snakes for help? Two of them were coiling past her at that very moment, but of course they didn't see her. Igraine hissed quietly, as she often did when she was feeding them, and took hold of one by the spines on its back.

'Hush,' she whispered as the snake reared its head back in alarm and bared its fangs, hissing. 'It's only me, Igraine. Take me to the small gate, would you? Quick!'

The small gate in the castle wall, the one that Sisyphus liked to use when he went down to the moat, was only a metre or so above the water. Apparently Igraine's grandmother always sank her jewellery in the moat there when enemies were approaching.

The snake easily carried Igraine through the water, but it wasn't necessarily taking the shortest route, and she saw in alarm that some of the soldiers were looking her way.

'So the Books of Magic will not be my reward if I win!'

cried Rowan the Heartless. 'But you still say that we are to raise the siege if I am defeated? What kind of a bargain is that?'

'Are you not said to be invincible?' the Sorrowful Knight called back. 'If you are, why should the price I ask for victory concern you?'

'And anyway,' called Albert, 'there'll be a reward for you too. Of course. If you win I'll turn every spear-point and every sword outside this castle into pure gold. Your greedy master would like that, wouldn't he?'

A murmur ran through the ranks of the besiegers. Osmund frowned, and whispered something to his castellan.

'Very well, I accept your challenge!' cried the Spiky Knight. 'When the sun touches the treetops of the wood, I will meet you outside the castle, and before the sun has set I'll have sent you tumbling in the dust.'

'That's what you think!' muttered Igraine. The snake had reached the gateway at last. It raised its head, tongue flickering, and reared up out of the water until Igraine was just outside the little gate. She quickly found a foothold on the ledge below it, and luckily she was still invisible under the soaking-wet dragon skin, but when she tried to open the gate her heart missed a beat.

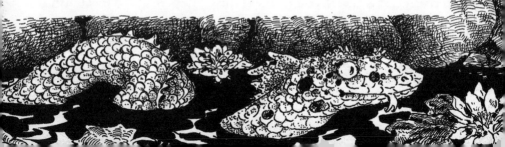

It was locked.

It's never kept locked! thought Igraine. Never! She desperately rattled the iron handle, though that didn't help at all, and finally her foot slid off the wet ledge. In alarm she grabbed for the dragon skin, but it had already slipped off her head and Igraine stood in front of the closed door, clinging to its handle, and watched her cover float down the moat.

'Look!' cried one of Osmund's soldiers, pointing his lance at her. 'There's a knight in silver armour trying to get into the castle.'

The archers immediately took arrows out of their quivers. Two soldiers drew their heavy crossbows. Now we'll see what this armour is good for, thought Igraine, as she went on shaking the handle.

'Stop!' she heard Rowan Heartless shout. She'd have known his voice among thousands. It was cold as mist. 'Don't shoot!' he said. 'That's the little minx, can't you see?' He thrust a couple of soldiers aside with the hilt of his sword and made his way through them until he was opposite Igraine on the other side of the moat. 'Were you planning to go on a little outing or to run away, girl-knight?'

'Leave my sister alone, Hedgehog!' Albert shouted down from the wall. 'If you hurt a hair of her head I'll turn you into a real hedgehog, roast you on a spit and serve you to our cat!'

Heartless just cast him a scornful glance. 'You terrify me, jug-eared brat!' he shouted. 'Can't you hear my knees knocking? Once we've captured this ridiculous castle I'll put you in a cage like a monkey and take you to Darkrock with me.'

'An interesting idea!' Albert called back, crooking three fingers unobtrusively and pointing them Igraine's way. The lock of the gate clicked. Once, twice. And before Igraine could fling all the insults she had on the tip of her tongue back at the Spiky Knight, the gate swung open, and a gust of wind that smelled very much like Albert blew her roughly through the open door.

A Squire for the Sorrowful Knight

'**M**y word, that was a close shave!' sighed Albert as he dried Igraine's wet armour in front of a magic fire. 'And all your cat's fault too. He kicked up such a fuss in your room that I let him out, but Father didn't want him eating any more knight-fish – because after all he's planning to turn them back into men again once this stupid business is over – so I locked the gate! How was I to know you'd be coming back that way?'

'All right, all right,' muttered Igraine, pushing a strand of dripping hair back from her forehead. 'No harm done.'

They were sitting near the main gate in one of the turrets on the battlements. Bertram and the Sorrowful Knight were on watch up on the wall, but at the moment all was calm outside the castle. Perhaps Osmund was tired of letting Albert make a fool of him, for the time being – or alternatively he was sitting in his tent thinking up a few brand-new nasty tricks. Whatever the reason, Igraine was glad of the silence.

'We had a terrible fright when Bertram came back without you,' said Albert, undoing a knot in the tail of one of his mice. 'Luckily he remembers magic spells better than you do, and he got the stone lion to open its mouth. When we heard about the fix you were in, your friend the sighing knight had the idea of distracting Heartless's attention by making his challenge right away, to give you a chance to escape. And it worked. But jumping into the moat like that . . .' Albert shook his head. 'You've always been so impulsive, little sister.'

'You're right.' Sighing, Igraine shook a tiny fish out of her shoe and threw it through the window and back into the moat. 'I'm sorry about the dragon skin.'

'Don't worry,' said Albert, blowing the magic fire out. 'The water snakes will fish it out.'

They were just imagining what their parents would turn Osmund into – currently Albert favoured the idea of throwing him and his castellan into the moat as a pair of particularly fat fish, and then letting Sisyphus loose on them – when the Sorrowful Knight hesitantly joined them.

'So the lance really was enchanted?' he asked.

Igraine nodded. 'Oh, yes. But Albert's powder put out the green glow. So you'll have your first fair fight with him this evening – and I'm going to be your squire!'

Albert rolled his eyes and left them alone without another word. The Sorrowful Knight, however, folded his arms and looked down at the place that Osmund's men were preparing for the single combat.

'You would be an excellent squire, no doubt about it,' he said. 'And I thank you with all my heart for the offer, but a knight without honour can manage without a squire too. Truly, you have shown enough proof of your courage. And your brother and your parents will need you this evening.'

'Not half as much as you will!' replied Igraine, picking a few water-lily petals off her armour. 'You can talk as much as you want, I've made my mind up. I'm going to be your squire whether you like it or not. There's nothing you can do about it! I'll hand you your lances, catch your horse if she throws you, make sure Osmund doesn't go casting any spells – and if the Spiky Knight tries any nasty tricks,' she added, as her lips began to tremble, 'then . . . then I'll push him off his horse with my own hands. I will, as true as you can call me Fearless Igraine. Because we're friends. Aren't we?'

Once again the Sorrowful Knight looked down at the tilting ground where he was to fight the Spiky Knight, and for a moment Igraine thought she saw something like a smile on his lips. 'Yes, we're friends,' he said, 'and what I call you is Brave Igraine. So you shall have your way. You will be my squire, and I'll try to prove myself worthy of your service.'

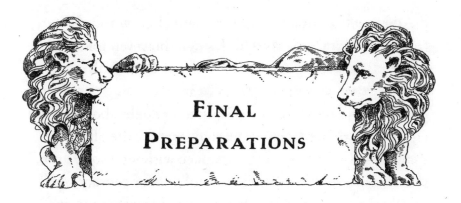

FINAL
PREPARATIONS

Sir Lamorak and the Fair Melisande almost got their curly tails in a twist when they heard about their daughter's latest idea. But what could they do about it? They knew Igraine, and they were well aware that there was no point in forbidding her to do anything when she made the face that said: *I'll do it anyway, even if I have to climb out of the tower window.*

Bertram just shook his head on learning of her decision, and muttered something like, 'No surprise there, then!' As for Albert, he tapped her armour and said, 'I just hope this stuff is as good as the books claim. Keep your visor closed and never look Osmund in the eye. Don't forget, he is a magician, if not a particularly good one.'

The sun was moving across the sky, the shadows were lengthening, and the magic concoction was slowly changing into thousands of tiny, shimmering globes that hopped about like popcorn, while Igraine's parents and all the Books of Magic kept trotting around it, sometimes clockwise, sometimes anticlockwise. You could get quite dizzy just watching them. The books sang and sang until their little voices were hoarse, while Bertram prepared the bath-house.

Down below the castle, the sound of weapons had died away again after a few half-hearted assaults on the drawbridge. It had taken Albert only a weary snap of his fingers to deal with those. Everything was going as the Sorrowful Knight had hoped: Osmund's soldiers were hanging around among the tents, doing nothing, while Rowan Heartless's squires prepared the tilting ground. Osmund had ordered all fighting gear to be moved away from the area between the tents and the moat, but it had taken hours to smooth the churned-up ground. Now a large rectangle had been marked out on the empty space, with torches burning on all four sides, and on the side nearest the camp the squires had put up a wooden platform adorned with Osmund's banner and his coat of arms.

Albert and Bertram were watching these preparations from the battlements, but Igraine was searching the armoury for lances for the Sorrowful Knight. She found five jousting lances in working order, and asked Albert to cast a spell to remove the rust from her great-grandfather's best sword. That much magic must count as fair play – after all, the knight had broken his own sword on the drawbridge. Then she carried it all down to the Great Hall where the

Sorrowful Knight was sitting under the portraits of her ancestors, cleaning his helmet.

Igraine put the sword on the table in front of him, and took the helmet from his hands. 'I'm afraid this is the best blade I could find,' she said. 'And polishing helmets is a squire's job.'

'If you say so!' The knight smiled, and swung the sword through the air to try it out. 'My word, not a bad sword. But with a good many notches on the blade. Your great-grandfather must have fought many a battle with it.'

'Yes, he did, I've read all about them in the family histories.' Igraine picked up Sisyphus, who was rubbing restlessly round her feet. 'My great-grandfather Pelleas was always having to protect his friends the dragons from other knights, and back then even the king was trying to steal the Books of Magic.'

'Indeed? Then it's time this sword saw some use again, don't you agree?' The Sorrowful Knight put the old sword back in its sheath. 'How high is the sun now?'

'Just above the wood already. It will soon be time.' Igraine looked at the portrait of her great-grandfather. He was smiling. He was the only one of her ancestors who smiled down at her from his golden frame. The other great-great-great-grandmothers, grandfathers, great-aunts and great-uncles all looked terribly serious and important. Pelleas's squire was in the picture too, a small, stout young man whose breast was swelling with pride as he held a jousting lance. Not long now, and Igraine herself would be a squire following her knight to the tilting ground. But it was quite different from the way she'd imagined it night after night in her dreams. The knight she served wasn't going to fight in a royal tournament, yet there was so much more at stake than just a kiss from a princess. If the Sorrowful Knight was defeated too quickly, all would be lost: Pimpernel Castle, the Books of Magic . . . and her parents, she supposed, would be running around with curly tails for the rest of their lives, unless something even worse happened to them. What would become of Albert, of Bertram, of Sisyphus, of Igraine herself? She held Sisyphus tight and pressed her face into his grey fur.

'Don't go!' he purred, and his amber eyes looked anxiously at her. 'You're only twelve.'

'I must go,' she whispered into his pointy ear.

The Sorrowful Knight put his helmet on and went up to her.

'Well, the time has come,' he said. 'Are you sure you won't stay here with your brother after all? I really don't need a squire, believe me.'

But Igraine simply shook her head without looking at him, and put the cat down on the tiled floor. 'Sisyphus, go and tell my parents that we're just setting out.'

The cat rubbed his broad head against her knee and ran away.

Igraine and the Sorrowful Knight, however, walked

through the great empty hall to the gateway leading outside. It was dark in the castle courtyard. The light of the sun, now low in the sky, hardly came over the high walls. The Sorrowful Knight reached the flight of steps and turned to Igraine.

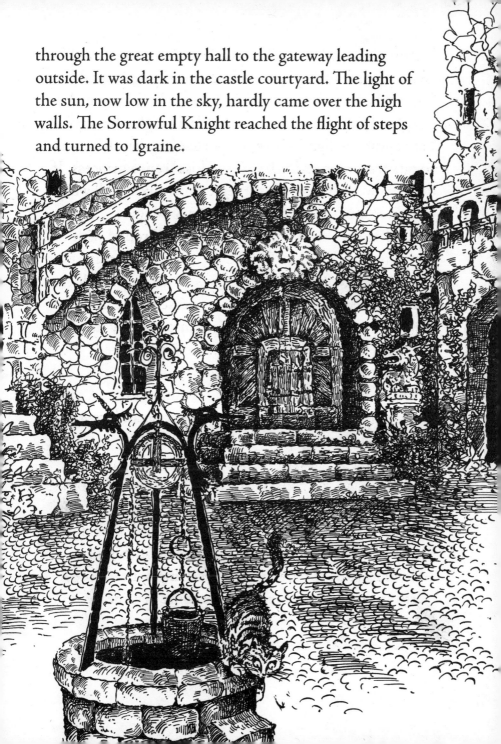

'It distresses me, Brave Igraine, to think that you will be the squire of a knight without honour,' he said quietly, 'in a fight that is probably lost already.'

'You can't know that,' replied Igraine. 'You were defeated three times by an enchanted lance. It's all going to be different today, you just wait and see.'

As they went down the steps to the yard, the two pigs put their snouts out of the tower window.

'Good luck, honey!' called the Fair Melisande. 'The enchanted bath is ready.'

'So if all goes well,' grunted Sir Lamorak, 'we'll be ourselves again by the time you come back. As you know, we only need an hour. Do you think you can distract Osmund's attention for an hour, noble knight?'

The Sorrowful Knight bowed low. 'I will do all that is within my power,' he replied.

'They're ready down there too!' Albert called from the walls. 'The Iron Hedgehog is already mounting his horse. You'd better get into the tunnel.'

'So be it. Let us go,' said the Sorrowful Knight to Igraine.

'Promise me not to do anything silly again, honey!' Melisande called from the tower.

'And leave your hot head here!' cried Albert. Bertram just waved. He was too fearful for her to say a word.

'See you later!' called Igraine. She blew them all a kiss, put the lances under her arm and dragged them to the entrance of the tunnel. The Sorrowful Knight pushed aside the stone slab and clambered into the dark hole. Before Igraine followed, she looked round once more.

'Look after yourself, Sisyphus,' she called to the cat as he watched uneasily from the tower window. Then she heaved the lances into the passage and, like the knight, disappeared down the tunnel that had been her great-grandfather's escape route.

THE KNIGHTS IN
SINGLE COMBAT

When Igraine and the Sorrowful Knight
climbed out of the stone lion's mouth, they
could already hear the fanfares in Osmund's
camp announcing single combat. The Sorrowful Knight
whistled softly, and his grey mare emerged from among
the trees as if she had been waiting for him there. She
was not alone. Lancelot was with her. He had burrs in his
mane and dirt in his coat, but he looked very happy, and
nuzzled Igraine in greeting.

She lovingly stroked his muzzle and swung herself
up on his back. 'Things are going to get exciting,' she
whispered to him. 'I just hope no one recognizes you.'

The torches around the tilting ground were lit, although
dusk was only just falling, and Osmund's soldiers formed
a double rank lining their path as they entered the camp.
Osmund was already enthroned in his armchair on a dais
put up specially for him, surrounded by servants and
some of his knights, and Rowan Heartless was waiting in

the middle of the space that had been marked out for the combat. His horse was harnessed and decorated as if for a great tournament, and he himself wore a huge blood-red plume on his helmet.

'So I see you come creeping through the back door again!' he called as the Sorrowful Knight and Igraine rode towards him.

'Did you expect us to let down the drawbridge so that Osmund the Greedy could take Pimpernel without a fight?' replied the Sorrowful Knight, reining in his horse just in front of Osmund's platform. 'Remember you gave your word, Osmund!' he called up. 'Every one of your soldiers is my witness. If your knight is defeated, you will lift the siege. He who breaks his word loses his honour.'

Osmund folded his arms. 'My knight will not be defeated,' he replied. 'And let's have no more talk; let's see you fight.'

Without another word, the Sorrowful Knight rode to his place. There was no coat of arms or banner displayed there, only a lance sticking in the ground. Igraine reached into her belt and took out a small bundle.

'I know you took your coat of arms off your armour because of your lost honour,' she said quietly. 'So I've brought my great-grandfather's banner. It used to fly outside his tent at every tournament. May I tie it to that lance?'

The Sorrowful Knight smiled. 'Do what you feel you

must, squire,' he said quietly.

So Igraine unfurled the banner of Pelleas of Pimpernel. It had got rather stained over the years, and Albert had had to cast a spell to mend several moth-eaten holes, but it was still very handsome. The coat of arms showed a beaver sitting on a golden book, with a snake coiled around the tree trunk next to it. Igraine tied the banner to the lance in the ground with a golden cord, and then rode her horse to stand beside the Sorrowful Knight's mare.

'Here we go,' murmured the knight, and he closed his visor and sat up very straight in the saddle.

'Who's your squire?' Rowan Heartless called to them. 'Not that little minx, is it? I'll overlook the fact that she's on a horse, which is no place for a squire. And although she's wearing armour, that doesn't bother me. But since when have girls been allowed to act as squires? I thought you set such store by the rules of chivalry, ever-Sorrowful and Sighing Knight?'

The Sorrowful Knight opened his visor with a furious jerk.

'You know the rules that matter to me very well!' he called across the lists. 'The rules of honour are these: Protect the weak. Never covet what belongs to someone else. Use your strength and skill in arms only in honourable competition. Never, never break the word you have given. And do not strive for power for power's sake. Those are the rules of chivalry by which a knight lives.

And anyone who lives by them, whether a man or a girl, should be accorded the honour due to him or her. The girl at my side certainly deserves to be honoured more than you or your predatory master.'

Rowan Heartless's pale face twisted in mockery. 'I am no squire whom you must instruct in the rules of chivalry,' he replied. 'If that little minx wants to play your squire, very well.' He closed his visor. 'There's only one thing I want to do now, and that's to fight.'

Without another word he dug the spurs into his horse, rode to his squires, and took the lance from the first squire's hand.

Igraine felt her hatred for the Hedgehog like a stone in her stomach. With shaking hands, she too gave the Sorrowful Knight his first lance.

'You gave me your word, Brave Igraine,' he whispered. 'Stay exactly where you are, never mind what happens.'

'Yes, all right,' whispered Igraine, and looked around. Osmund's soldiers were crowding around the tilting ground, and beyond them, behind the battlements over the castle gate, she saw Albert and Bertram. The two of them looked tiny – and very, very far away. And suddenly, for a split second, Igraine was afraid she would never get back to Pimpernel. The castle looked so small and dilapidated behind all those soldiers. The stone lions were hanging their heads on their ledge, the gargoyles' eyes were closed and they were snoring. Igraine thought she could hear them herself, even with her helmet on. But Osmund didn't seem to notice any of that. He had eyes only for the tilting ground – as the Sorrowful Knight had planned.

At a signal from Osmund, four servants raised their trumpets and blew a fanfare announcing the first joust.

Heartless and the Sorrowful Knight put their lances under their arms, settled in the saddle one last time, and rode their snorting horses into the fray. The two men galloped towards each other over the dusty ground. Their armour clinked, the horses snorted under the weight of the armed riders. The plume on the Spiky Knight's helmet shone red as fire. When the points of their lances were only the length of a horse's stride apart, Igraine held her breath and Osmund leaned forward in his chair.

Rowan Heartless's lance struck the Sorrowful Knight's armour with a fearful crash. But the Sorrowful Knight had hit his opponent too, right between the spikes of his suit of armour. Both riders swayed in the saddle, but neither of them fell. Furiously, Heartless flung his splintered lance down in

the dust before riding back to his place. One of his squires scurried forward to take it away. The Sorrowful Knight, however, carried his own split lance back to Igraine himself.

She was horrified to hear how heavily he was breathing. 'Are you wounded?' she asked, worried.

But the knight shook his head. 'No,' he managed to say. 'And that will surprise Heartless, since he always unhorsed me at the first tilt before.'

Rowan Heartless, back at his own end of the tilting ground, was shouting at his squires, kicking out at them with his armoured foot, and rejecting all the lances they offered him.

'He's looking for the lance with the green glow,' Igraine whispered to the Sorrowful Knight. He was sitting perfectly still on his horse beside her, with his visor open, as he watched his opponent ranting and raging. Igraine gave him the second lance.

Osmund was looking nervously at his champion. Finally Rowan Heartless snatched a lance from the hands of one of the squires, gave it a suspicious look, and stuck it under his arm. Angrily, he slammed down his visor and rode his horse back into the tilting ground.

The sun was slowly sinking behind the wood. Darkness was falling, but the light of the torches illuminated the empty space marked out between the tents and the castle.

Up on the castle wall, Albert summoned glow-worms

to light up the battlements. Green light spilled from the tower window.

Once again, Osmund's servants blew their trumpets. And for the second time the two knights urged their horses forward. Soon they lowered their long lances. Each iron tip swung up and down, pointing at the breast of the oncoming knight. Once again Rowan Heartless just managed to get his blow in first, but his aim was not good. His lance glanced off the Sorrowful Knight's armed shoulder. Meanwhile the Sorrowful Knight struck Heartless in the middle of his chest with his blunted lance. The terrible blow made the Spiky Knight sway so much that only gripping his horse's mane kept him in the saddle.

A murmur ran through the throng of soldiers crowding around the tilting ground. They were even sitting on the catapults that had been cleared away, the wreck of the battering ram, anywhere they could get a good view of the fight. Osmund the Greedy, up on his dais, folded his arms and angrily chewed his beard. His weakened castellan straightened himself with difficulty, rode back to his squires, swaying, and beat them about the ears with his splintered lance. Igraine couldn't make out what he was shouting, but she saw two of the squires run to their master's tent.

'He still thinks they've just given him the wrong lance,' she whispered when the Sorrowful Knight was back beside her. When he opened his visor she handed him a scarf so that he could wipe the sweat from his face. 'You were wonderful!' she said. 'I've never seen such a good lance-thrust before.'

'Don't exaggerate,' said the knight, but he couldn't help smiling once again. 'He's furious,' he added quietly. 'So furious that he's making mistakes. That's good from our point of view – very good.'

'The light in the tower is getting brighter and brighter,' Igraine whispered back. 'The magic can't be much longer now. So don't take too many risks. What's more, we have only three lances left, and one of them is a bit wobbly.'

At that moment Heartless's squires came back with two new lances. The Spiky Knight examined them both and then flung them angrily to the ground.

Igraine laughed softly. 'Look at that! Any moment now he's going to realize that he doesn't have an enchanted lance any more. What do you think?'

But the Sorrowful Knight didn't answer. He looked down at his horse in concern, made the mare take a few steps forward and back again. Then he patted her flank, which was wet with sweat, and bent down to Igraine.

'Listen,' he said in a low voice. 'I'm going to have to ask Heartless to continue the combat with swords, on foot. My mare is lame. I must spare her. If Heartless will not agree to my request, he'll probably unhorse me with his lance at the next tilt, because I won't be able to ride to meet him fast enough. But have no fear, heaven knows it wouldn't be the first time I land in the dust. I'll go on fighting on foot, and if Heartless acts honourably he will dismount from his own horse and finish what we've begun with the sword. If he doesn't, I'll have to try pulling him out of the saddle by his lance.'

Igraine looked at him in alarm, but there was no time for her to protest. Rowan Heartless was already waiting, his horse restlessly pawing the dust. When the Sorrowful Knight rode out too, everyone could see that his horse was lame. The grey mare was limping on her right foreleg. The Sorrowful Knight signalled to his opponent to meet him in front of Osmund's dais. Terrified, Igraine watched them talking. When the Sorrowful Knight returned to his place, he glanced briefly at Igraine and shook his head. Her heart almost stopped.

For the third time a fanfare blew for the next tilt; for the third time the knights lowered their lances.

Sir Lamorak had taken Igraine to a tournament twice, although he hated all that fighting business. And she had been to some other tournaments with Bertram. She had eagerly awaited every tilt with her heart beating fast, so excited that she couldn't sit still for a second. She had climbed up on the bench to get a better view and cheered when a knight fell in the dust.

But everything was different in this fight.

Igraine didn't want to watch. She just wanted to close her eyes; she wanted it to be over. This time her heart was beating fast, but not with excitement. She suddenly knew only too well what fear felt like. Terrible, breathtaking fear. The snorting of the horses hurt her ears, and when the lances crashed as they struck the knights' armour Igraine clenched her fists so tightly that her fingernails cut into her hands.

The Sorrowful Knight took his lance under his arm once more, even more firmly than before, and raised his shield to ward off the lance-thrust of his opponent, who was racing towards him, but just then the grey mare's lame foreleg gave way beneath her. She shied and threw him out of the saddle. At the last moment Rowan Heartless raised his lance and made his horse swerve to avoid a collision with the stumbling mare. But the Sorrowful Knight fell on the trampled earth with a clatter of armour. Staggering, he got to his feet again, and Igraine was alarmed to see him put a hand to his shoulder. The grey mare limped over to him and nuzzled him, but at a sign from him she hobbled back to Igraine with her head lowered.

Rowan Heartless was still astride his horse with his unused lance in his hand. He was staring down at his fallen opponent without any visible emotion.

Not a sound was to be heard from the watching soldiers. Osmund had risen to his feet. Is all lost now? Igraine wondered, glancing at the castle. Her parents still weren't standing on the battlements, as she had hoped.

But the tower was shining as if the stones themselves were glowing green.

Suddenly Heartless sat erect in the saddle, spurred on his horse, and rode towards his challenger. The Sorrowful Knight was steady on his feet again. He had drawn his sword, the blade that had once belonged to Igraine's great-grandfather. For a moment Igraine thought Heartless was going to attack the Sorrowful Knight with his lance and ride him down into the dust. But before she could draw her sword and urge Lancelot into the lists, the Spiky Knight reined in his horse and threw the lance to the ground.

A murmur ran through the ranks of the watching soldiers as he dismounted and drew his own sword.

In the torchlight, the blade looked as if it were made of fire. The two knights stalked stiffly towards each other. By now the sky above them was black as pitch, and only the slender moon stood in the sky over Pimpernel.

The swords clashed with terrible force, again and again. Igraine jumped nervously at each stroke. She closed her eyes, opened them again, clutched her own sword in both her hands, which felt far too weak to lift it, and waited for her heart to break with fear.

The two knights were fighting ever more fiercely. But the swords were heavy, very heavy, and soon their strokes were less certain and missed their mark. One or other of the combatants was forced down on his armed knee more and more frequently, and they both found getting up increasingly difficult each time. Their gasping and groaning rang in Igraine's ears. There was not another sound to be heard in the night. And then, suddenly, Heartless raised his sword for a fearsome stroke. The Sorrowful Knight parried it, forced his opponent back and drove him backwards with a flurry of sword-strokes, until Heartless lost his balance, stumbled and fell. Gasping, he lay on his back, right in the middle of the tilting ground. His sword had fallen from his hand and was too far away for him to reach it – and the Sorrowful Knight put the point of his own sword to his opponent's breast.

'We won!' shouted Igraine, so loudly that for a moment everyone turned to her. Osmund made use of that moment. He leaped up, went to the edge of his dais, and spread his fingers. Hardly anyone noticed, but Igraine recognized magic when she saw it, and she knew at once why the Spiky Knight's sword was sliding back to him over the trampled ground. Without thinking of the promise she had made the Sorrowful Knight, without thinking of what she had promised her parents and Albert either, she swung herself up on Lancelot's back, galloped into the tilting ground and brought the horse to a standstill right above the enchanted blade. Snorting, he set one front hoof on the great sword.

'Call your squire off!' roared Osmund. 'You're breaking the rules, Sorrowful Knight!'

'You're the one who's breaking them!' Igraine shouted back. 'Since when do swords start moving of their own accord without magic?'

Osmund did not reply.

A murmur rose among his soldiers.

The Sorrowful Knight, however, took the point of his sword away from the Spiky Knight's breast and straightened up.

'You are defeated, Rowan Heartless,' he said. 'Get up and go away with your greedy master. But first tell me where you are hiding the noble ladies who were entrusted to my care.'

Heartless rose to his feet with difficulty. His heavy armour, weighed down by all those iron spikes, made him stagger, and when he opened his visor his face was white with rage.

'You haven't defeated me!' he shouted at the Sorrowful Knight. 'No one defeats me. The little minx there has cast a spell on me, that's the only reason why you brought her! She's a magician like the rest of her family.'

'That's not true!' cried Igraine indignantly. 'You wicked liar! You were going to save yourself by magic. You and your greedy . . .'

But she got no further.

'Seize her!' cried Osmund. 'Seize them both and put them in chains.'

Igraine looked round in alarm. Some of the soldiers

were hesitating, but enough of them were ready to obey. They came storming into the tilting ground from all sides, with lances, spears and drawn swords. Lancelot pranced on the spot and threw up his head. Igraine looked desperately up at the castle. The tower was dark, the whole place was dark, she couldn't even see Albert on the battlements.

'Flee, Igraine!' cried the Sorrowful Knight, fending off the first soldiers trying to seize him.

'Leave him to me!' roared Heartless, snatching a sword from the hand of one of the men. 'Let me pass, he's mine!'

'The knight can wait. Bring me the girl!' Osmund called to him. 'Bring her to me alive, understand?'

Heartless swung round, a furious retort on his lips, but Osmund stared at him until he bowed his head.

Igraine saw him coming towards her. She struck out with her sword at every hand reaching for her, fended off spear-points, kicked helmets and breastplates. Lancelot turned in a circle, neighing shrilly, kicked and bit, but however hard Igraine tried to get him close to the Sorrowful Knight she simply couldn't do it. The stallion was far too agitated, and the milling throng around her was growing denser all the time. She had to watch helplessly as the Sorrowful Knight was thrown to the ground, and the next moment Heartless was standing in front of her.

'Well, little minx!' he cried. 'And how do you like the

life of chivalry? Not quite the same thing as playing on the battlements in a shiny suit of armour, is it?'

With a single blow he struck Igraine's short sword from her hand, pulled her out of her saddle, and threw her over his shoulder like a sack of beans. She tried to bite him – his fingers, his nose, his ears, anywhere – but he was protected by his chain mail and his armour. Laughing, the Spiky Knight carried her to Osmund's dais and threw her at his master's feet. Igraine tried to scramble up, but two of Osmund's servants forced her back on to her knees.

'Excellent!' cried Osmund, looking down at her with a mocking smile. 'And now your silly brother will bring us those books in person. He won't be able to let the drawbridge down fast enough, if that means getting his captured little sister back. And when your foolish parents are home from their journey,' added Osmund, pulling at his beard with satisfaction, 'then they won't find a castle standing here any more. As for their children, well, I have yet to decide what I'm going to turn you two into.'

'Here's the other prisoner, sir!'

Igraine spun round.

Three soldiers were forcing the Sorrowful Knight down on his knees in front of Osmund's dais. They had torn the helmet off his head.

'Osmund, you have no honour,' said the knight wearily. 'You have broken your word. Nothing could be more disgraceful.'

'Oh, yes, it could. You brought an enchantress with you as your squire,' replied Osmund scornfully. 'That's truly disgraceful. You're the knight without honour.'

'I'm not an enchantress, you dirty liar!' shouted Igraine, trying to bite Osmund in the knee, but he stepped back just in time.

'I think I'll turn you into a gnat,' he said. 'Or a yapping puppy. And your magician of a brother will make an excellent donkey.' Raising his hand, he signalled to his soldiers. 'Take these two to Darkrock and throw them into the Dungeon of Despair. Her brother will have to bring me the books in person if he wants his sister back. I'm sick and tired of sleeping in a stuffy tent outside this crumbling castle.'

But just as the soldiers were hauling the two prisoners to their feet, a bright flash of lightning shot across the sky.

It came from Pimpernel, shot down from the castle battlements, ran zigzag over the tilting ground, and struck Osmund's armchair. Coloured sparks flew through the air, and all of a sudden, instead of the chair, Albert stood there life-size on the wooden dais. Blue fire dripped from his magic coat, the little bells on its hem were ringing, and three mice were sitting in his dark hair.

ALL IS REVEALED

Albert's big entrance struck everyone silent. Osmund was so scared that he would have dropped into his armchair, except that it wasn't there any more.

'Osmund, Osmund,' said Albert. 'You are indeed the shiftiest and most dishonourable creature going about on two legs. Oh, and greetings from my parents. They're just back from their journey, and they'd like your fire-raisers and book-robbers to know they'll spend the rest of their miserable lives as cockroaches, scurrying about outside our castle, unless they unchain my sister and the noble knight, right this minute.'

Osmund was not the only one who turned to stare uneasily at the castle on hearing Albert's words. White fire was spraying down from the gargoyles' mouths into the moat, and up on the battlements stood two figures whom none of the besiegers had ever seen before.

A few of the soldiers, their fingers trembling, began

undoing the bonds that held Igraine and the Sorrowful
Knight captive, but their lord and master obviously hadn't
yet taken in the gravity of the situation.

'Stop that!' thundered Osmund, in such a loud voice
that the soldiers flinched back in alarm. 'What are you
waiting for? Grab that jug-eared beanpole!'

Albert spread his arms wide and smiled, the way he did
when he'd left a big fat spider dangling over Igraine's bed.
Fire danced along his arms, over the backs of his hands
and down his fingers. Even his hair was sprinkled with
tiny flames. 'You're in trouble, Osmund,' he said. 'Real
trouble, and if you don't know what that means you're
about to find out.'

Igraine freed herself from her half-loosened bonds, and
helped the Sorrowful Knight to undo his. No one was
taking any notice of them. They were all staring at Albert.

'Seize him, by Death and the cauldron!' shouted
Osmund.

But his soldiers didn't budge.

Thunder rolled behind them, making their hair stand
on end under their helmets, and another flash of lightning,
followed by a third, flickered across the black sky. Two
shining white globes struck the ground at Osmund's feet,
smoking hot and scattering sparks, The lightning was
so bright that everyone, even Igraine and the Sorrowful
Knight, had to close their eyes for a moment. When they
could see again, Sir Lamorak and the Fair Melisande

were standing beside Albert. Igraine's father was carrying Sisyphus, and two Books of Magic were sitting on her mother's shoulders.

Osmund stared at those books so greedily that they put out their tongues at him.

'Allow us to introduce ourselves, Osmund,' said Sir Lamorak politely. 'I am Lamorak, also known as Lamorak the Wily or Lamorak the Witty, and this is my extremely clever and, as you can see, extremely beautiful wife Melisande.'

'We,' said Melisande, taking a step towards Osmund, 'are the parents of this jug-eared young man and the girl in silver armour there. And as I am sure you can imagine, we are not particularly happy about your treatment of our children, let alone your dishonourable behaviour towards the noble knight who is facing you now. Thank you very much,' she added, giving the Sorrowful Knight her most beautiful smile, 'thank you very much indeed for your truly chivalrous aid.'

The knight bowed, looking embarrassed.

As for Sir Lamorak, he turned to Osmund again.

'The fact is,' he said, 'we are rather annoyed, as you will soon find out for yourself. Books, page 232, please. *Da capo, fortissimo!*'

The two books began to hum. It sounded like the angry buzzing of a couple of hornets. Igraine had never heard them sing such notes before.

Tiny flames flickered up Osmund's dais, surrounding him with a wreath of fire and then creeping down from the platform like a burning fuse on their way over to Rowan Heartless. The Whispering Woods began to rustle so loudly that the night was filled with an eerie roar, and the water snakes slithered out of the moat and wound their way, hissing, across the tilting ground and towards the tents.

Osmund's soldiers groaned in terror. They retreated from the flames, but now here came the snakes. In panic, they stumbled into one another, trod on each other's feet, pushed and shoved just to get away – but get away where?

The men ran off in all directions, anywhere but towards the place where the snakes were coiling around the tents with their tongues darting in and out. Cries of fear drowned out the rustling of the forest, and soon Osmund was alone on his dais. Only Igraine and the Sorrowful Knight were left on the now deserted tilting ground – and a few steps away from them, grim-faced and with his sword drawn, stood Rowan Heartless.

The books were still humming, a deep and angry note, and now it sounded like bumblebees buzzing in two-part harmony.

The Fair Melisande pushed her dark hair back from her forehead and placed her fingertips together. Then she said softly:

'Wicked evil, black as night,
Now be empty, airy, light!
May the earth of you be free,
Let it not infested be
By such cruelty and greed,
Be gone, away from here, make speed!
Treacherous miscreants, be off!
Melisande has had enough!'

Light as a couple of balloons, Osmund and his castellan champion floated up into the air. However much they kicked and struggled, flailed their arms about, cursed and swore, they couldn't get back to earth. They hung in the air as if invisible hands were holding them there.

Igraine couldn't resist it. She went over to Osmund and gave him a push which sent him spinning around on his own axis like a top.

'Now, now, my dear,' said Sir Lamorak, hugging her tight. 'We mustn't take advantage of our prisoners' unfortunate situation. That's not chivalrous, is it?'

'You're right,' said Igraine, burying her face in his robe. It still smelled very slightly of pig bristles and the stable.

'That's what bothered me most about being a pig,' said Melisande, putting her arm round Albert's shoulders, 'not being able to give my children a hug.'

'You miserable magicians!' Rowan Heartless almost turned a somersault as he drew his dagger from his belt and sliced the air with it.

Shaking their heads, Igraine's parents looked at each other. 'What are we going to do with them, dear heart?' asked Sir Lamorak.

'Throw them in the castle moat,' Albert suggested. 'Sisyphus will soon fish them out again, won't you, Sisyphus?'

The cat expectantly licked his whiskers.

'No way!' said Igraine, picking him up. 'They'd only give him indigestion. And they'd certainly bite my fingers when I feed the snakes. No, you'll all have to think of a better idea.'

At this Osmund and Heartless were perfectly still. Obviously they were worried by their conquerors' suggestions. Only the Sorrowful Knight had said nothing so far. He stood there holding his injured shoulder and looked up without a word at his enemies dangling in the air.

'I think you ought to decide what happens to them,' said Igraine, taking his hand. 'You've had more trouble with them than anyone.'

But the Sorrowful Knight shook his head. 'I don't want revenge,' he said. 'I just want an answer. Where are the three ladies? Did you kill them, Heartless, or are you keeping them prisoner in some dark place?'

They all looked up at Rowan Heartless.

But he only smiled mockingly. 'You'll never find out,

sighing knight!' he said. 'However long you look, you'll never find them.'

At this point Albert went over to him, looked up, and smiled his broadest, typical Albert smile.

'That's not very friendly of you,' he said. 'But then you never were very friendly. Now that I come to think of it, you were always an extraordinarily unpleasant person. Not much nicer than your bungling magician of a master. But we have plenty of time. We'll leave Sisyphus here to watch you while we go back to Pimpernel Castle for some supper. If you happen to remember the answer to this noble knight's question, just send us the cat. However, if you have visitors while we're gone, for instance all the peasants whose pigs and chickens you stole, or the men you forced to play soldiers for you, well . . .' Albert shrugged his shoulders. 'Well, then it could get rather uncomfortable for you. Not everyone's as peace-loving as we and this noble knight are. But perhaps you'll still be alive when we come back, who knows? We'll just have to see. Have fun, all alone in the dark.'

Albert turned and led Igraine away with him. 'Oh, my goodness, talking about fun . . . !' he said, turning back again. 'I do believe a few of your men are already on their way back. But I'm sure they love you so much for your kindness to them that—'

'Stop!' Osmund's voice was considerably shriller than usual. 'Go on, tell him!' he snapped at his castellan, giving him a kick that sent his spiky armour rattling. 'Give that miserable sighing drip his answer, will you?'

'No, darkness take it! I'll do no such thing,' snarled Rowan Heartless, jabbing his spiky armour into his master's side. 'I like listening to his eternal sighing far too much. Why don't you do something? What's the idea, leaving us hovering here, making us look like idiots to everyone? I thought you were such a great magician!'

Osmund made no reply to this.

'At the moment he's not a magician at all,' Sir Lamorak replied for him. 'I took care of that. And as to whether he was ever a great one – well, opinions may differ on that point.'

Rowan Heartless cast his helpless master a scornful glance. 'Be that as it may,' he sneered, 'even if your men carve us into slices I won't say where those ladies are.'

'Then I will!' shouted Osmund. He was paddling so frantically in the air that his shoes fell off. 'They're in the tent! His tent!'

Igraine looked at him disbelievingly.

'Liar!' she said. 'I've been in his tent myself. There aren't any ladies there. I'd have noticed.'

Heartless stared down at her as if he couldn't believe his ears. 'What are you talking about, minx?' he growled. 'You've never been in my tent.'

'Of course she has,' said Albert, speaking up instead of Igraine. 'She broke the spell on your lance. Why do you suppose it didn't help you to win your fight this time?'

For the first time a little colour rose to Rowan Heartless's pale cheeks. 'You just wait, minx!' he said. 'When I get back on the ground again—'

'Which I guess isn't going to be for quite a while yet,' Igraine coolly interrupted him.

Her father gently picked up a mouse that had jumped off Albert's head on to his, and put it on his shoulder. 'Well, well, Osmund,' he said with a deep sigh. 'So now you're trying to lie to us. How shabby of you. I think we really ought to go in for supper, as Albert suggested.'

With the mouse on his shoulder, he went to the edge of Osmund's dais. 'Come along, my dear,' he said, giving Igraine his hand. 'You must be ravenously hungry after all your heroic deeds.'

'I wasn't lying!' bellowed Osmund. 'The three ladies are in his tent. I turned them into birds. That's what he wanted.'

Igraine stood still, thunderstruck.

'Birds?' she asked.

'Yes, birds, I said so!' Osmund was waving his arms about so vigorously that he suddenly found himself hanging in the air upside down.

But Igraine turned to the Sorrowful Knight. 'He's not lying after all,' she said. 'I saw those birds. But there were four of them.'

THE THREE LADIES
FROM THE MOUNT
OF TEARS

They all went to Rowan Heartless's tent: Igraine
and the Sorrowful Knight, Albert and their
parents, but they left Osmund and his champion
the Spiky Knight where they were, dangling up in the air
with Sisyphus guarding them. The cat wasn't very pleased,
until Melisande conjured up a bucket full of fat fish that
persuaded him to stay put.

It was dark in the Hedgehog's red tent, pitch dark, but
Albert, Sir Lamorak and the Fair Melisande were still
covered with sparks from the magic lightning, and in their
soft light the falcons on their perch were clearly visible.
They were sitting hunched up with their heads under their
wings. Once again the smallest falcon was the first to be
on the alert, spreading its wings as it had when Igraine
slipped past it before, and it uttered such a raucous cry
that the other three brought their heads out from under
their feathers too.

'You see?' said Igraine. 'Four falcons! Perhaps the one

that keeps getting so worked up is the only real bird!'

'Perhaps.' The Sorrowful Knight went over to the birds and took the leather hoods off their heads. Bewildered, they blinked in the strange light that filled the tent.

'Noble knight,' said the Fair Melisande, putting her hand on his armed shoulder, 'your courage gave us the time we needed to return to our former shape. Now let us help you.'

Incredulously, the Sorrowful Knight turned to her. 'You think that you could break Osmund's spell?'

'Definitely,' replied Sir Lamorak. 'Ordinary magic is considerably easier to reverse than magical mistakes, you know.'

The Fair Melisande gently moved the knight aside, stood in front of the perch with the birds on it, and took the smaller of the Books of Magic off her shoulder. As soon as she sat it on her left hand it began humming quietly.

The falcons jerked their heads, alarmed, and listened to the strange sound.

'Page 4,' said Melisande, and the book opened at a page that was covered all over with illustrations of tiny, colourful animals, birds and insects. They were crawling, leaping and fluttering over the letters on the page as if they were alive.

Melisande closed her eyes, raised the book a little

higher in the air, and said in a voice that was hardly any
louder than the whispering of the wind:

> *'Be what once you were, you birds,*
> *What you were so long ago.*
> *Let me help you to remember,*
> *You wore no feathers, well you know.'*

The thin golden perch broke like a rotten twig under
the weight of the four ladies who were suddenly sitting
on it. Yes, four. They landed with a bump on the carpet
that Rowan Heartless had spread on the floor of his tent.
When the confusion of skirts and veils had died down, the
Sorrowful Knight helped his three lost ladies to their feet,
with a happy smile on his face. But Igraine put out her
hand to the fourth.

'My word, Baroness!' she said, helping the old lady up
from the carpet. 'What on earth are you doing here?'

With a deep sigh, the old Baroness of Darkrock pushed
her tangled grey hair back from her forehead and looked
down at herself.

'All present and correct!' she said, relieved. 'Thank
goodness. No more feathers, no claws on my toes.' She
felt her face a little anxiously, and sighed happily again on
discovering that she had a nose there instead of a hooked
beak.

'My dear Igraine,' she said, tapping her smartly on the

helmet and looking stern. 'Couldn't you have broken that horrible spell on me this morning? Didn't I flap those wretched wings hard enough when you were stumbling round me?'

'But how was I to know it was you?' asked Igraine. 'How come you let your own nephew enchant you?'

Embarrassed, the old lady picked a feather off her dress. 'I thought he was quite nice,' she murmured. 'I have to admit I was wrong.'

'Yes, indeed,' said Sir Lamorak. 'According to Bertram, Osmund poured all your stock of honey beer into the moat at Darkrock. Granted, that will be good for your teeth, but—'

'He did what?' the Baroness interrupted. 'Where is he?'

But Sir Lamorak had turned his back to her, for the other three ladies were shyly plucking his sleeve.

They looked very like each other. All three had golden hair and were almost the same size, they wore beautiful but very impractical dresses, and they had tiny feet which would not be much use for running away from Spiky Knights.

'Noble sir!' said the tallest of the ladies, as the other two smiled very sweetly. 'We owe you and your wife our infinite gratitude. If you wish, my sisters and I will serve you to the end of our days. Perhaps you need childminders for your son and daughter, or . . .'

Albert and Igraine looked at each other in dismay.

'No, no, that won't be necessary, really it won't!' Albert interrupted the lady hastily. 'My little sister does need supervision, it's true, but I can take care of that myself. And as for being rescued, you owe that almost entirely to this noble knight. Word of a magician's honour!'

Looking embarrassed, the Sorrowful Knight bowed his head. 'I allowed Heartless to steal you away,' he said, without looking at the ladies. 'I hope you will forgive me. I was not worthy to be your knight.'

'Oh no, there he goes talking nonsense again!' muttered Igraine, but her mother gave her a warning look and put a finger to her lips.

'Of course you're worthy!' cried the three ladies. 'You defended us most chivalrously! What could you do against such deceitful magic?'

'Learn a little magic himself, maybe,' Albert whispered to Igraine.

However, the three ladies went up to the Sorrowful Knight, and one by one they kissed his dusty cheek.

Igraine suppressed a groan.

'Escort us back to our castle,' said one of the ladies. 'Be our protector again.'

The Sorrowful Knight bowed very, very deeply to her.

'I will be happy to escort you back,' he replied. 'But I won't stay, for my skill in arms is not enough to protect you from magic and treachery. So I have decided to learn some new arts, and to study, if they will allow me,' he said, turning round, 'with the noble Sir Lamorak and the Fair Melisande, and not least with their extremely clever son Albert. In return, I offer to instruct your noble and very brave daughter Igraine in all the skills that a chivalrous knight must learn.'

All at once Igraine's heart felt so light that she almost floated up to the top of the tent.

'An excellent idea, er, Sorrowful Knight,' said Sir Lamorak. 'And we offer you our services with the greatest pleasure, don't we, my love?'

'Oh, yes.' The Fair Melisande nodded. 'But on one condition. Now that you are no longer a Sorrowful but, I hope, a Happy Knight, you must tell us your real name.'

'I was once known as Sir Urban of Wintergreen,' said the Sorrowful Knight, 'and I will go by that name again.' And with these words he turned to Igraine. 'What do you say, squire?' he asked. 'Will you come with me when I escort these three noble ladies back to their castle? After all, I am a knight with honour again, so I need a squire now.'

Igraine looked at her parents. 'Of course. I'd love to!' she said, and the Fair Melisande and Sir Lamorak the Wily sighed – and nodded.

'Well, it would be a bit boring for you with just those three ladies, wouldn't it?' Igraine whispered to the Sorrowful Knight.

'What did your noble squire say?' asked one of the ladies.

Luckily Sisyphus came in at that moment, with a half-eaten fish in his mouth.

'Sisyphus!' cried Albert, astonished. 'What are you doing here? You're supposed to be guarding the prisoners!'

'Flown away,' purred Sisyphus, settling down comfortably on the carpet with his fish.

'What do you mean?' asked Albert in alarm, as the cat greedily smacked his lips.

'The wind blew them away,' replied Sisyphus. 'What did you expect me to do? Fly after them?'

Igraine's parents looked at one another in dismay.

'The wind – my word,' murmured Sir Lamorak. 'Never thought of that, did we?'

'Who flew away?' asked the Baroness, who was just reviving herself by sampling the Spiky Knight's provisions of beer.

'Your nephew,' replied Melisande, 'and his castellan.'

'Oh, were those two turned into birds as well?' asked the Baroness.

'No, no,' said Igraine, taking her hand. 'You see, it's rather a complicated story.'

So they all went back to Pimpernel Castle. Albert ordered the drawbridge to lower itself, which after some hesitation it did, and the Fair Melisande broke the spell on the moat. No sooner had she lowered her hands than twenty-five dazed men emerged from the water lilies. The snakes carried them to the bank, where Sir Lamorak and the Sorrowful Knight pulled them out of the water.

'The wind has blown your masters away,' said Melisande as they stood before her, dripping wet. 'The tents you see still standing there are empty. The siege is over. You can go home.'

Most of the men didn't wait to be told twice. They made off on their unsteady legs. But five men still stood there.

'What are you waiting for?' asked Albert impatiently. 'You can go.'

But the five just looked gloomily at the feet they had got back. 'We liked it down there,' one of them muttered.

'What?' said Sir Lamorak.

'We want to be fish again,' said a second man. 'It's a better life. Enough to eat, no one ordering you around . . .'

He looked longingly into the moat.

'I have a cat who eats fish,' said Igraine.

But that didn't seem to bother the men.

So Sir Lamorak granted their wish. He turned the five of them back into fish, and then, with the help of the Books of Magic, he and the Fair Melisande conjured up such a banquet as Pimpernel Castle had never seen before, with not a crumb of biscuit or a blue egg in sight. Albert entertained the three ladies until late into the night, getting his mice to do tricks for them, and Igraine finally had her chance to tell the Baroness all that had happened since her twelfth birthday.

The only part of the story she wasn't telling yet was how she had stolen the Baroness's favourite horse . . .